"A fast-paced, yet touching story depicting the realities of dog racing through a Greyhound's eye."

—*Christine A. Dorchak*
President and General Counsel
GREY2K USA

Daisy's Greyt Escape
Copyright © 2011 Jeff Scott

ISBN 978-0615544656

Daisy's Greyt Escape

Jeff Scott

Printed in the United States of America

Chapter One

A hush hung over the Blue Arrow Racing Park, even though the two-tiered grandstands were jam-packed with hundreds of spectators. Many people sat on the edges of their plastic seats, basking under the yellow glow of the stadium's blazing lights. Others pressed binoculars against their eyes. Everyone waited.

Suddenly, the sound of a buzzer shattered the silence. Eight Greyhounds blasted from their starting boxes like cannonballs and tore after a fake white rabbit fastened to the end of a mechanical arm. Dirt, clay and sand sprayed into the air as fur scraped against fur.

While the elusive rabbit motored along the rail on the inside curve of the track, the dogs chased it at a blistering pace. Many of the spectators shouted and clapped, watching the thundering hounds soar around the oval track at forty miles an hour.

At the final turn, the Greyhounds whisked around the curve and sprinted toward the finish line in an explosive fury. Each dog zipped over the line in quick succession to the roar of the crowd. But Priscilla, a petite white and black dog, crossed far behind the others. After coming to a halt, she glanced into the grandstands and heard some people booing at her. One man even pointed at her and yelled. Priscilla dropped her head and sauntered farther down the track to cool off with the other Greyhounds.

Very early the next morning, a blue van with two sprinting Greyhounds painted on its side, rolled to a stop next to a white industrial-looking building—one of three wooden structures where the racing dogs lived on the track grounds. A man's shadowy figure stepped out of the van and plodded toward the kennel door. A cold mist softened the clanking of a leash and harness that dangled from his fingers.

The kennel door creaked open and the man slipped inside. The pale light of dawn revealed the name *'Willie Sharp'* stitched onto a uniformed shirt that matched the color of the van.

"Row three, number twenty-two," he whispered to himself. "Gotta be down here."

Willie tiptoed past crates of sleeping canines. At the end of the aisle, Priscilla stirred. She raised her half-closed eyes and fixed them on Willie's silhouette. He drifted closer and closer.

When Willie's face became clearer, Priscilla's eyes ballooned. At the same time, a faint strip of daylight from a high, narrow window highlighted the leash and harness as Willie lifted them to his waist.

Willie halted in front of Priscilla's crate and peered inside. His protruding, scrubby red beard made him look years older than his actual age of thirty. The glare from his piercing eyes forced Priscilla to roll up in a ball in the corner. Her back paw vibrated against the metal bars and her teeth chattered as she released a faint cry.

Then Willie unlatched Priscilla's crate door. He reached in with the harness and slipped it over the hound's head.

"No! I don't wanna go anywhere," Priscilla howled as she pressed her body against the back of the crate. "I'll run faster next time."

Willie frowned, obviously irritated by Priscilla's whimpering as he slid the harness over her ears and down her thick neck.

"Get up!" Willie waved a finger an inch from the dog's snout. "You better make this easy for me."

Priscilla whimpered again as the man clasped the straps around her deep chest. Then he clipped the leash onto the harness' metal ring. With a powerful tug, he pulled Priscilla through the crate door and into the aisle. By now, several dogs in the kennel were awake. Some yowled. Others barked.

"Help me! Irving, help me!"

"Quit your yapping." Willie gripped the leash tighter. "Can't stand whining dogs."

On the other side of the room, Irving, a black dog with white blotches on his back and neck heard the racket and woke up in his crate. He shook his head, expelling the remnants of sleep, and looked through the maze of crates. He rocketed to his feet. His eyes bulged in rage as he watched Willie drag Priscilla up the aisle and toward the door.

"Oh, how I wish I could understand what this man is saying," Irving moaned. "Maybe then I'd know where he's taking Priscilla."

"Give me another chance." Priscilla flopped onto the floor. "I'll race better."

Willie kicked her in the rear and yanked her back onto her feet. Priscilla gave up the struggle and shuffled behind as Willie opened the door. Just before she stepped out, Priscilla swiveled her head and located Irving's crate. Their terrified eyes met for a second. Willie jerked on the leash and pulled Priscilla onto the pavement. The door slammed and the rumble rattled several crates.

Out in the parking lot, Willie swung open the van's back doors and pointed inside the cargo area.

"Get in, loser!"

Priscilla trembled as she craned her neck and peered inside. The smell of gasoline wafted into her nostrils. Just before Willie could kick her again, she hopped in. Willie unclipped the leash and shoved her further inside.

"Irving! Irving!" Priscilla cried just before Willie slammed the doors.

Inside the kennel, Irving cocked his ears and listened to the muffled whines. He heard the engine start up. Then he furled his brow and backed up a step. With a snort, he rushed forward and rammed his head against the crate door. He backed up a step and rammed it again. Then again. Finally, he crouched down. A few tears trickled down his long muzzle just as he buried his head underneath his blanket.

Chapter Two

A year after Priscilla was shipped away, thirty Greyhounds were running, rolling, and playing inside the track ground's sand-covered exercise yard. Several sniffed the clover along the four-foot aluminum fence while a few smelled each other. A chubby track worker tossed foam soccer balls to a couple energetic dogs. At the same time, a blue racetrack van stopped at the entrance gate. The track worker jogged over to the gate and opened it. The van backed in.

All the Greyhounds looked up. Some galloped to the gate and formed a semi-circle. The cab door opened. A boot crunched onto the sand.

Daisy, a pretty, light-brown and white Greyhound, stood next to Irving in the corner of the yard. Her gaze was glued to the van. Irving stared at her, indifferent to the commotion at the gate.

"Last place, Daisy," he said. "Two races in a row."

"Hey! Here come some new arrivals." Daisy's eyes flickered with excitement.

"And you can still sleep at night?"

"Give me a break, Irving. It's not every time."

Irving also looked over to the van. His pupils narrowed as he saw Willie shut the cab door.

"It doesn't *have* to be every time," he said.

Willie raised his chin. He tightened his jaw and scanned the dogs as he thumped a stick on his palm. The nearest Greyhounds knocked into each other and scattered. Willie walked around the van and opened the back doors. From inside the van, he pulled out a six-foot long catchpole with a rope noose at one end and leaned it upright against the open door.

"Out! Out! I ain't got time for you to lounge around."

Willie lifted his stick in a threatening pose. Four Greyhounds darted from the cargo area and scurried into the yard. A fifth dog hesitated. Willie swatted him on the rear. The dog clambered down and ran off.

Meanwhile, the chubby track worker had closed the gate. He then checked the latch, making sure it was secure, to prevent any curious Greyhounds from wandering off.

"Hey, boss," he called out. "I see we got the newbies in to replace the dogs from the past week."

"Those slow losers." Willie held his stick out at arm's length and sliced it through the air several times like a sword. "Don't they realize we're trying to run a business here?"

"But Mr. McKenzie isn't gonna like you hitting the new dogs. You know how he feels about—"

"Then how else does he expect me to get them in line, Rick? He wants me to be head dog handler, well, this is how—"

Suddenly, Rick pointed inside the van. "Hey, you got a straggler still in there."

Willie whipped his head around and glared inside the cargo area at a white, muscular Greyhound.

"Okay, big shot, get down."

The Greyhound stepped to the edge. He lifted his head high and glanced around the yard, just like Willie did seconds before.

"You want me to drag you out with this, Tommy?" Willie nodded at the catchpole.

Tommy looked at Willie and smirked. "Well, well. Does this man think he's in charge?"

"Stop barking and get yourself out of there." Willie pretended to reach for the catchpole.

Tommy leaped down, knocking over the catchpole. The pole smacked Willie on the head. Willie rubbed his forehead, picked up the pole and tossed it in the van. When he turned around, he noticed a couple Greyhounds staring, as if mocking him.

"Whaddya lookin' at?" he said through clenched teeth.

Rick stepped closer to Willie. "I heard your Uncle Marty offered you a job at the animal control in Cedartown. Gonna take it?"

"What?" Willie rubbed his forehead again. "And work some place where I ain't top dog? Not happening."

"I don't know about you," Rick said. "But I'd think animal control would be a bit more exciting job than here."

Rick reopened the gate while Willie returned to the cab and started the engine. He leaned his face out of the open window.

"I've done my share of scooping up after dogs. If you think that's fun, why don't you take the job?"

Meanwhile, in the middle of the exercise yard, Tommy winked at two female dogs as he strutted past them. Then he noticed Daisy and fired off a wink at her too. Her ears shot up and she smiled back.

The two female dogs grinned at Tommy and then looked at each other.

"I haven't seen a hound like him for a long time!" one said.

"Oh, yeah." The other dog took a big step toward Tommy. "I think I'll—"

"Hey, it's my turn." Her peer also moved a foot forward but abruptly stopped. "Rats! Here comes Milady. She did it to me again."

A Greyhound with silky, gold fur leaped into Tommy's path.

"You gotta be real fast." Milady looked at Tommy's sleek, agile frame.

"They call me Turbo Tommy. You win many races too?"

"All the time. They call me Magic Milady because it seems I suddenly appear over the finish line."

Tommy smiled and nodded. "I love girls with lots of speed."

In the corner of the yard, Casey wandered over to Daisy and Irving."

"This time she's Magic Milady?"

Daisy smirked with pride as she continued to stare at Tommy. "But when he sees how fast *I* am, it'll be me walking alongside him, not Milady."

Irving spun his head away from Daisy and released a dull groan.

"Ha!" Casey said. "They should call you Dragging Daisy. Or, Lazy Daisy. When was the last time you even came close to winning a race?"

Daisy's face became serious. "But that will change."

"Poor, simple Daisy." Casey shook her head. "Never getting enough attention."

Casey stuck her nose in the air. She let out a huff and marched away as Daisy scowled back. Meanwhile, Irving's forehead crumpled as Tommy and Milady walked over. Milady looked at Daisy and shook her head.

"Another race tonight, Princess."

Daisy pivoted her head and glowered at Milady. "I can't wait. This time you'll be left in the dust."

Milady turned to Tommy. "Ever since she got here three months ago, that's all I've been hearing. She can only win in her dreams."

Milady burst out laughing just as the Greyhounds heard a whistle blow. This was the signal for the dogs, especially those that were taking their time, to return to the kennel—the exercise session was over. Milady and Tommy strolled off. Daisy spun her head to face Irving. But he was already gone, joining the other dogs heading away. Daisy also ambled toward the kennel behind all the other dogs but paused when she heard a distant bark.

Daisy curiously gazed past the kennel and toward the parking lot where a red Corvette whizzed across the asphalt. An Afghan Hound's head jutted from the window. Its tongue and long, silver-blond hair waved in the breeze. Then the dog lifted his snout and released several joyful-sounding howls.

Daisy's face beamed with delight as she watched the car circle the parking lot a couple times and then speed out of the track grounds and onto the road. Her gaze followed the car as it banked around a curve and disappeared over a hill. Then a second whistle blew. Daisy's cheerful expression vanished as she was plunged back to reality. She hung her head and sauntered toward the kennel.

Chapter Three

That evening, there were several races scheduled with Daisy's being the final race. When the sun was low in the sky, the stadium's lights switched on, filling the air with a dazzling flash. Eight muzzled Greyhounds, each with a different colored and numbered blanket hanging over their backs, paraded single file in view of hundreds of dog racing fans. This was a track regulation to show that the dogs are healthy enough to run. Just before they entered their starting boxes, Irving nudged through the crowd of dogs and track workers.

"Daisy!" Irving made sure his voice was barely above a whisper as the other Greyhounds jostled around him. "You need to get this into your head. These people could get rid of you if you don't run faster. You must try harder tonight. How many times do I have to beg you?"

"C'mon, there'll be a lot more races." Daisy turned and waltzed toward her starting box. "I feel great tonight. Relax."

Irving backed up a step and stared at her as she passed by. He shook his head and trudged into his own box.

Milady also stepped into her box, one slot to Daisy's left.

"It's about that time again for you to try and beat me, Princess." Milady let out a loud chuckle as a few other Greyhounds restlessly howled and pawed the ground inside their boxes.

"Yeah, you'll see—Tommy will see. I'm gonna..."

"Now, now, no one likes a liar."

Daisy gritted her teeth and planted her feet firmly on the starting box floor. No sooner had she done that than the deafening buzzer sounded over the stadium.

The Greyhounds blasted from the boxes and sprinted after the fake rabbit in hot pursuit. Daisy bolted down the front stretch with a surge of confidence. Her coat instantly became a blur under the track's radiating lamps. A broad smile tore across her face as she pulled into second place, four body lengths ahead of Milady.

At the second turn, Daisy felt her hind legs tingle. Then they buckled. It was the third race in a row that her muscles felt strange. Milady saw her chance and exploded through a gap to catch up. She fired off a sneer as she passed Daisy.

"Bye-bye, Princess," Milady shouted, as sand shot into Daisy's nostrils.

After the third turn, Daisy was near the back of the pack. Her tongue flagged to the side of her cheek. She dug her paws deeper into the packed sand as the dogs jockeyed for position rounding the fourth turn. Gloom gushed through her veins and drove out the last few drops of her power. Her heart sank further into despair when she imagined how much more attention Tommy would give to Milady.

As the end of the five-sixteenth of a mile race came into view, Irving and Tommy rocketed neck and neck toward the finish line. It seemed like their gangly front legs would snap off with each stride. But Tommy stretched his head and beat Irving by a nose. Milady and Porter zipped over the line after them, followed by Teddy and Dalton. Daisy hobbled over in seventh, barely ahead of Casey.

Daisy halted and stomped her paw. Casey also stopped. Both struggled to suck in air as a track worker took off their muzzles and racing blankets.

As Daisy was catching her breath, she gazed over the stands and watched several hundred people shuffle into the concrete aisles and head toward the exits. The aroma from a few lonely hotdogs sizzling at a nearby food stand continued to drift thickly through the air.

Casting her thoughts about Tommy aside, Daisy felt a cold chill race across the fur on her back. She knew that some Greyhounds had been mysteriously taken away in the past and that most dogs never wanted to talk about where those unfortunate ones went. But once in a while, a rumor would surface that those taken away came near last place for many weeks.

"Lucky!" Casey said, gasping. "You got just plain lucky."

Daisy was jolted from her thoughts. She turned and gave Casey a look that said, '*That was lucky?*'

Willie saw the two dogs yapping and ran out onto the track. He pointed a bony finger.

"Get moving down there!"

The two dogs immediately obeyed and trotted to where the other dogs were cooling off. Milady saw Daisy and galloped over.

"Wow!" Milady's face beamed. "You had a brilliant run. Think Tommy noticed?"

Tommy stood several feet away, his lungs still heaving after his victory. He raised his ears when he heard his name and trotted over to Milady.

"Looks like it was our Princess who got left in the dust," Milady said to Tommy. She then glared at Daisy. "Let's go, Tommy. I don't have time for losers."

"Maybe they should call her the Pitiful Princess," Tommy added.

Tommy and Milady burst out laughing and walked off. Daisy's head sagged until her nose skirted the ground. She ambled in the opposite direction. Irving spotted her and loped over.

"That was a horrible run," he said. "What's wrong? You had a great start."

"It's only one race." Daisy kept her head down, too ashamed to look Irving in the eye.

Irving stepped closer. "You think these people are gonna let that slide? You still lost badly." He took a swallow of air. "But there should be another race in a couple of nights. You'll have to do better then."

"It's no use. Forget it."

"Why are you giving up?" Irving's voice became high-pitched. "You used to do much better and you're still young. What's the problem?"

"My legs keep getting stiff." Daisy pawed at the hard, brown dirt.

Irving took another deep breath. "Haven't I been making things clear? If you don't do better, you may not last here much longer. Do you remember how they took Jasper away last week?"

"Jasper?"

"That skinny black and brown dog."

"I thought he had strained his foot and would eventually be back."

"He wasn't hurt. He just couldn't run fast anymore. I've seen a lot more than most dogs because I've been here so long." Irving became silent when he saw Casey, still wheezing and coughing from the race, stumble toward them. He waited until she passed by.

"I see the pattern." Irving drew closer to Daisy and lowered his voice. "The men come into the kennel, usually in the morning, and take one of the dogs out of its crate. Sometimes it's after exercising like with Jasper. But every dog taken alone like that was always racing terribly."

Daisy watched Casey hobble away. "Then they should train the slow dogs to run better and give them another chance."

"Ha, they wouldn't waste their time." There was a heavy pause as Irving's eyes narrowed. He glared at a track worker picking up hamburger wrappers and racetrack schedules that had blown onto the track.

"There's always more new dogs coming that will race better than those who have gotten slow."

"Why wouldn't you warn Jasper or other dogs—especially if you saw the signs?"

"I did warn some dogs, but not for a long time."

"What made you stop?"

Irving quickly looked around. Most dogs had cooled and were drifting back to the kennel.

"Well, I haven't warned anybody since..." He closed his eyes and sighed.

"Since when?" Daisy asked.

Irving dropped his head. "Not since they took my sister away."

"You had a sister here?" Daisy cocked her head and returned a confused look.

A tear sneaked down Irving's cheek. "It's been a year since I've seen Priscilla."

"I really don't want to hear this." Daisy wheeled her body and trotted away. Irving opened his eyes. He rushed forward and pounced in front of Daisy to block her retreat.

"Listen to me! You're gonna know because you're in the same situation." Irving let out a deep sigh and then spoke in a calmer voice. "For some reason, Priscilla couldn't get any faster. And then that terrible day came when she was taken from her crate. I wished with all my heart I could've taken her place. She needed me and there was nothing I could do."

Daisy gaped at Irving as her legs began to tremble.

"Soon after we came here," Irving continued, "I warned her to improve. I pled with her constantly. Then she started to avoid me, especially when she came in last place a couple of times."

"Did you tell her that she could be taken away?"

"Yeah, but she didn't think it would happen so soon."

Daisy raised her head and glanced into the darkening sky. The first stars had appeared as dozens of white moths danced around the lights that circled the track.

Irving took a step forward. Daisy dropped her head and he looked hard into her eyes.

"We don't know what these people are thinking or what they're going to do next. If I knew, I would've tried much harder to convince Priscilla sooner. I should've screamed at her, I should've—" Irving paused when two dogs glanced over at him.

"What could you do?" Daisy lowered her voice. "You tried your best with her."

"No. I didn't try hard enough, at least not near the end. When she didn't speak to me, I just left her alone."

As Irving finished those words, a track worker blew a whistle. The Greyhounds galloped toward the kennel, except for Daisy and Irving.

"I didn't even say good-bye." Irving turned his quivering head to hide a few more tears.

"Maybe they take these dogs back to the place where we learned to run? Remember? It was so much more fun back then."

"I don't think there are any warm soapy baths where they end up."

"How can I run faster?" Daisy moaned. "This is hopeless. What should I do?"

She stared at Irving and wondered why he wasn't moving toward the kennel. He stood there, like he had suddenly been transported to another time and place. Then Irving looked down at Daisy's legs and gave a slight nod. He quickly lifted his head and gazed into her eyes with a tenderness that she had never experienced before.

"There *is* something you can do," Irving finally said.

"Tell me!" Daisy pounded her paw on the ground. "I have to know how to run faster."

"This is not hopeless. I've got a secret."

"A secret?" Daisy's heart hammered. "How can anyone have a secret when we're all kept so close together in those cramped cages?"

"I did because I *had* to keep it a secret."

"Why are you just telling me now?"

"Because I thought a time would come when I would have to help another dog I...I cared about."

Irving looked beyond the track's seven-foot green border fence and into the dark woods. The silhouettes of massive oaks and maples reached high into a copper sky. His thoughts were interrupted as Porter rushed over.

"Let's go guys, didn't you hear the whistle?"

Porter ran back to the kennel. Daisy and Irving followed several yards behind.

"Quick!" Daisy said. "What's the secret?"

"No time now. Find me in the yard tomorrow."

Daisy and Irving squeezed among the dogs funneling into the kennel.

"Then you'll let me know how I can run better?" Daisy asked.

Irving stopped. The last two dogs skirted past him. Then he leaned close to Daisy's ear.

"Shhh. This has *nothing* to do with racing." Irving swung around and headed to the crates with the other dogs.

Daisy stood at the doorway with a stunned look. Then she turned and poked her head through the doorway to look back at the racetrack. She wondered what secret Irving could possibly be keeping. At the same time, a stiff breeze played with her ears. Then the wind became stronger. She closed her eyes and let her tongue hang out, just like the Afghan Hound did in the Corvette earlier that day.

A smile sprinted across Daisy's face and, for several seconds, she seemed adrift in another world. Then Willie showed up in the doorway holding a large bag of dog food on his chest. He never saw Daisy. He tripped over her and plunged to the floor. The bag split open and thousands of nuggets scattered in all directions.

"You, stinkin' beast!" Willie lay sprawled across the floor. He tried to get up, but the nuggets were like marbles and he slipped again and went down even harder.

Daisy's tail coiled under her belly as she retreated to her crate. Meanwhile, laughter erupted throughout the kennel as the dogs watched Willie trying to get to his feet—and ending right back down again.

Nothing to do with racing? Daisy kept thinking. She hustled into her crate as another track worker latched the door behind her. *What else could it be?* Daisy lay on her blanket and with her chin between her front paws. She replayed Irving's words over and over in her mind while each Greyhound was put back into its crate for the night.

Suddenly, a chorus of yapping canines erupted when a track worker came into the kennel with a bucket of chicken-flavored biscuits. Apparently, Willie's mishap wouldn't prevent the dogs from their nightly ritual of getting a bedtime snack. A minute later, Daisy lifted her head and watched the man slide the treat between the bars of her crate. She stared at it. Normally, she would have gobbled it down in the blink of an eye. Instead, she put her head down again with the biscuit an inch from her nostrils.

What could he possibly know? She took a nibble.

After the lights went out, Daisy lay with open eyes. It would be another two hours before she finally drifted off to sleep.

Chapter Four

The next morning, the sun's rays pried through the row of tiny windows high above the kennel floor. Several dogs yawned and stretched in a narrow band of light on the far wall. Two track workers came in and banged on top of the crates to wake up the rest. Daisy suddenly awoke. She rolled onto her side and felt the leftover biscuit. Then all the memories from the previous evening came roaring back into her mind—especially that there was a secret she needed to hear.

The workers unlatched the crate doors and a stream of restless dogs sandwiched through the aisles and to the outside. As soon as they swarmed onto the exercise yard's white sand, Daisy spotted Irving and rushed over to him. Irving saw her coming and walked to a place a good distance from any of the other dogs.

"Tell me." Daisy jumped from one side of Irving to the other. "What's the secret?"

"Don't show your excitement so much." Irving glanced over each shoulder. "The other dogs will wonder what's got into you."

"Okay, okay." Daisy stood still but her eyes shone with intrigue. "Quick, what is it?"

Irving again looked around. "I also had a brother here at the track."

"Are you going to tell me all about your parents and grandparents? C'mon, what's this secret that has nothing to do with racing?"

A foam soccer ball bounced across Irving's feet. Seconds later, two Greyhounds tore after it and plowed between Daisy and Irving. After they passed, Irving stepped closer to Daisy.

"There were three of us from the same litter that came here. When Priscilla was taken away, Everett got really heartbroken and he kept getting slower and slower.

"Slower than me?"

"Almost. But I couldn't wait until they also took him. I had to do something, so..."

Daisy's eyes became round and she hopped on her toes.

"...I helped him to escape from this miserable place."

Daisy's mouth opened wide. "You what? How?"

Irving slowly glanced to his right. Daisy followed his gaze until it came to the green fence that circled the track grounds. Irving raised his right eyebrow and a smile dashed across his face.

"You mean—wait a sec—that *fence*? He got over *that*?" Daisy's ears flickered and shock oozed from her eyes. "But those fences are real high. I think they're like that so no one can get out of here."

"That's what these people think." Irving's eyes glittered and he let out a snicker.

Daisy's forehead crumpled as she pondered what Irving had just told her. "So that's why you kept it a secret. When you knew that another Greyhound was in danger of being taken away, then you could let it know ahead of time how..." Daisy stared at Irving and felt as if her jaw had plunged into the ground.

A long pause followed.

"Are you crazy? You want me to escape over *that* fence?"

"Not just you. We. I'm going too. It's either escape or be taken away."

Daisy gaped at the fence. Her tail curled underneath her belly.

"How could *any* dog get over that?" she asked. A look of despair washed over her.

"Let me tell you," Irving said. "Just after a race, Everett and I got out of sight from where the other dogs were cooling off. Then he ran towards the fence and jumped as high as he could. But it wasn't quite enough. He ended on top of the fence. His belly got all red and scratched—it was terrible to watch. Then he fell to the other side. I still shudder when I recall the sound of him hitting the ground."

"There must be another way," Daisy said. "Isn't there an open gate or something—just to walk through?"

"Don't even think of trying to get out of here through the entrance. The men have those..."

"What?" Daisy felt a flutter of anxiety. "What do the men have?"

"Never mind."

"What are you not telling me?

"Listen to me. This is the only way out. My brother did it, and we will too. You just need a little courage."

"And you think that's something I can just wish upon myself and I'll get?"

"You'll get courage when you realize there's a way to have a better life and not be kept in these cages twenty hours a day."

Daisy thought for a moment. "The track people must have known he got out."

"Yeah, but they didn't realize it until they took the dogs back to the kennel. By then, he was long gone. They didn't even bother keeping the Rottweilers out too long."

"Rottweilers?" Daisy felt a cold sensation stream through her body that was strong enough to make her ears fall against her head.

"Those two vicious, black dogs you sometimes see with the men. They are...well...let me finish about Everett."

While Daisy absorbed this tidbit of information that she would have rather done without, Dalton and Teddy wandered close by and began to roll on the warm sand. Daisy and Irving spun their heads.

"Let's move over there," Irving said under his breath, nodding toward an empty spot near the center of the yard. The two trotted across the yard and Irving went on with his story.

"Everett ran through the woods all night without stopping to rest. Then he saw the lights of a house that stood among the trees. At this point he didn't care if he was seen. He was so hungry and tired. Then he went to lie on the back steps of that house. He slept until the next morning but was awake real fast when a man opened the door and stepped out. Then the man brought him inside."

"So, he found a home?"

"Yep. The man fed him and let him sleep on a soft, clean blanket."

"Why didn't he return him here?" Daisy asked just as many of the dogs were gathering at the gate that led back to the kennel. They were hungry and eager to dive into their breakfasts, which would be waiting for them in their crates.

"Maybe the man thought he had been abandoned for a long time. Everett never knew why. Anyway, after another week, Everett got away from his house for a little while. He wanted to see if he could find his way back to the track."

"Why on earth would he want to come here again?"

"To let me know he had found a new home. Then, at other times, when the man would be away for the day, and Everett was kept in the enclosed part of the yard, he would jump over the fence, which, fortunately, is not as high as this one here. But he would never do this if his owner were home. Then he would take off, but always made sure to be back before he thought his owner would return."

"And none of the other dogs realized he had come around?"

"I wouldn't tell anyone. We couldn't risk having the Rottweilers find out."

"What are they all about? Just tell me."

Irving paused. A mask of worry clouded his face. "If they knew Everett came back, they'd tear him apart."

"Are those the dogs I sometimes see tied up by the vans out front?" Daisy asked. "They always scowl at me. I guess that's why getting out of here through the entrance is—"

"Not even a possibility," Irving quickly interjected. "If it weren't for those workers keeping them away, I think they would cause a lot of trouble. But don't worry about them now."

"One thing that still bothers me—how did you talk to your brother?"

"See where part of this area comes up to that green fence?"

Daisy looked over to the farthest corner of the yard.

"When we were outside once, Everett was waiting on the other side. He made a real high whining sound. It didn't even sound like a dog, more like bird.

But I recognized him. I went over there and we whispered through a crack in the fence."

"What a paradise," Daisy said. "Almost too hard to believe."

"He loves his home." Irving's face immediately glowed with exhilaration. "Nothing like these old, drafty buildings here. He has this large, round bed with a warm blanket on it."

"Like the black ones we have here?"

"Much softer. And cleaner too."

Daisy sighed. "It's hard to imagine that a dog could be that happy."

"Now we have that chance too." Irving pounded the dirt with his front paw. "We must take it!"

"Some of the Greyhounds have talked about dogs that live in places just like Everett but I assumed they were making things up. Irving, why are we in here? Why are there some dogs free and happy while the rest of us...?"

"We'll have that too." Irving gave her a supportive smile.

Daisy turned and looked across the yard at the track ground's parking lot. "I saw a dog riding in a car yesterday—completely free and happy. I'll bet he has one of those homes. That's the life I want."

Daisy and Irving then held each other's gaze for several seconds. Irving broke the stare and looked back at the fence.

"Only that fence stands in our way. If you want a real home badly enough, you'll get over it."

That night, after all the Greyhounds were asleep in the kennel, Daisy tossed and turned on her blanket for hours. Her stomach hurt. She grunted and moaned as she thought about how she could ever get over the fence. But drowsiness eventually overtook her and she fell fast asleep.

Daisy then had a dream that she was racing the race of her life and crossed the finish line far ahead of all the other dogs. Not even Tommy was close.

"I won! I won my first race ever!" Daisy's tail rocketed back and forth as the rest of the dogs made it to the end. She danced on her toes and stuck her nose into the air as Milady gave her a furious look.

As Irving, Tommy and some of the other Greyhounds came to congratulate her. Suddenly, all the dogs' ears perked up as a metallic voice came over the stadium's loudspeaker.

"We've just discovered that Daisy ran for the wrong reason—not to bring the track money, but to get Tommy to like her," the announcer said.

All the dogs looked at each other, then they glowered at Daisy in disgust.

"We disqualify Daisy," the announcer continued, "and make Milady the new winner. Daisy will be shipped away."

Daisy's mouth hung open as the other dogs laughed and mocked her. Then Willie took a leash and waded through the pack of Greyhounds in search of Daisy.

"Where's that dog?" he said with a snarl. "Where's that dog?"

Daisy burst out of her slumber. Willie's dark form floated up the aisle toward her. A leash and a harness swung by his side as he tiptoed past the snoring canines. He held a piece of paper as he read the name of each Greyhound from a tag on its crate.

"Where's that dog? Gotta be right down here."

Irving also woke up and saw Willie. He sprang to his feet as Willie halted a couple steps from Daisy's crate. She slowly glanced into his eyes. Willie looked down and sneered.

"Not me! Oh, not me!" Daisy jerked her head back.

"Don't touch her!" Irving pressed his nose against the crate bars and showed his teeth. "Don't lay a hand on her!"

Willie looked over at Irving. He raised the leash and slammed it on top of Daisy's crate to get Irving to stop growling. Every dog's head in the kennel snapped up as Irving lay back on his blanket. Willie took another step and stopped. Max, the Greyhound housed to Daisy's right, looked at her and shook his head.

"Guess it's your time, sweetie." Max closed his eyes and cradled his chin on his front paws.

Daisy squeezed her eyelids. Her body trembled and her teeth chattered in the dead silence of the kennel.

Chapter Five

Daisy's whole life flashed through her mind in an instant. She first saw herself when she was a puppy, hopping around with her littermates in the plush grass at the breeding farm. She remembered being bathed in the round metal basin, which was always filled with soapy water that smelled like the flowers that grew everywhere around the farm. Those were the happiest times in her life. She missed them the most.

Then she saw herself at her first training track where she turned into a grown-up dog. The races were usually shorter and her hard efforts were rewarded with tasty peanut butter biscuits.

And then the scene changed to when she was yanked away from her siblings and brought to the Blue Arrow Racing Park. The joyful times were over.

When Daisy's crate door didn't unlatch, she gradually opened one eye, then the other. Willie's back faced her as he opened Dalton's crate across the aisle from her. Lately he was doing poorly, having finished in last place three times.

Daisy's heart wilted and her ears flattened on the back of her head. Blood pulsed against her skull and a wave of heat blasted through to the tip of her tail as she listened to the wailing.

"I don't want to go! I don't want to leave! Someone, please help me!" Dalton twisted and wagged his head to prevent Willie from thrusting the harness over his head. It didn't work. Willie pulled Dalton's neck down. The harness glided over the dog's ears. Dalton grunted as Willie clasped the straps around his chest. He hauled Dalton out of the crate and muscled him into the aisle.

"I wish there was something we could do," Buddy moaned.

"Just be glad it wasn't you," Floe said as Dalton slumped onto the floor. "Such is the life of a racetrack dog."

"I'll try better next time! Give me another chance!" Dalton thrashed harder as Willie lugged him to the doorway. Just as Willie opened the door to drag the dog out of the kennel, Dalton grabbed the doorframe with his jaw. His teeth sunk into the wood. Willie yanked the leash and Dalton tumbled onto the pavement—a chunk of the doorframe still in his mouth.

Dalton gave up and followed Willie. The kennel door closed and Dalton's whimpering faded away.

All the dogs whispered among themselves but suddenly became like stones when the van doors slammed. Many of them had seen this happen once or twice, but for Daisy, it was her first time. She shook on her blanket and was unable to utter a peep as the sound of the van's motor gradually disappeared.

After Dalton was gone, none of the dogs spoke for several minutes. Daisy lay on her blanket as the blood drained back out of her face. A ripple of frost surged up her spine as she shuddered at the thought of what could have happened if they took her instead of Dalton. Several other dogs that had never seen a kennel mate taken away covered their eyes to hide their tears.

As Daisy recovered a bit from the shock, a thought came to her that plunged her back into despair.

Dalton finished sixth the other night, but I came in seventh place! If they did that to him, what are they thinking about me? No wonder that man was looking at me like that!

"What makes this so hard," Buddy spoke up again, "is that we don't know what happens to them."

"Didn't some of us agree that we wouldn't talk about this?" Jillian asked. "There's nothing we can know and nothing we can do about it. If they decide to take one of us away, what can we do to stop them?"

"But we should know." Buddy's voice echoed through the entire room. "It's our lives they're dealing with."

"Doesn't anyone here have any idea what happens to them?" Teddy asked with a tear in his eye. "I just came to this track. I didn't expect it would be like this."

"Get used to it," Hallie said. "Who told you living at the track would be a paradise?"

"So, this is how it all ends?" Teddy shook his head as the room became brighter with the rising sun. "After all that effort to show how good we are before coming here—to go like that?"

The kennel erupted as three dozen voices chattered at once.

"Maybe they get sent to another track?"

"Do you think they could be brought somewhere else to live? There are other dogs that live with people."

"But no Greyhound that left like that has ever come back to tell us where they were brought to."

"What can we do to find out?"

"They kill them all."

Every dog turned in the direction of Daisy's crate. The entire kennel was silent. No one had ever mentioned that word. The topic rarely came up, and, when it did, everyone was careful to dance around the rumor that the Greyhounds that left the kennel were destroyed.

"They simply get rid of dogs by killing them." All attention was on Max. He sat up in his crate. Max was one of the oldest dogs at the track. His eggplant-colored coat revealed a few strands of gray hair. There were also several bald patches across his back and thighs where the hair had rubbed off from years of lying in crates.

"You don't know that for sure!" Irving roared back from the other side of the room. "You should never say that, especially with the possibility that anyone here could be taken away next."

Daisy's ears sprang up as she crouched on her blanket. She was sure that Irving would show everyone that Max didn't know what he was talking about.

"They've been doing this for years," Max said more callously. "It's our fate. Why even discuss it? Besides, I'm tired of you all bringing this subject up. You got your answer, now leave it be. "

"But we're talking about our lives and the lives of those we care about," Irving said. "If we don't know the truth, then none of us should say what you just did."

Daisy stood up in her crate, as most of the others had done when Irving and Max began to argue. She felt that Irving might be responding on her behalf.

"It's a miserable place," Max added. "At least you get your biscuits."

Then Tommy yelled from a corner of the room. "But if everyone could run as fast as I could, then no one would fear being taken away."

"You'll slow down someday too," Max said. "No one can stay on top forever."

"You're old and weak," Tommy shot back. "That's why you've given up. Why don't you go next since you're not doing anybody here any good?"

Max raised his voice. "You won't listen to me? I know they take them away to destroy them."

"How do you know that?" Tommy was a bit troubled because Max seemed so sure. "How could you know that while the rest of us have no idea?"

"You don't want to know." Max's voice boomed from one kennel wall to the other.

"I want to know!" Tommy snarled and made a fake lunge toward Max. "You tell us right now.

"All right." Max grunted and cleared his throat. "I'm gonna tell you since none of you seems to believe me. I've been here longer than any of you, almost five years. When I first came to this track, there were other dogs here, but they weren't racers like us. People who worked here owned them. One day, a Greyhound was taken away and so I asked one of those Rottweilers what happened to them. At first, he didn't want to say, but after I bugged him for a while, he told me plainly. I was so shocked that I denied to myself for a long time what I heard."

"And what did he say to you?" Buddy asked.

"He said that after a racing dog has lost its worth to the track, they are put to sleep, as he called it. But I knew what he meant. I was horrified. I asked other Greyhounds that had been at the track before me if it were true. They didn't want to answer me. That told me enough. From that moment forward, I knew it was win or die." Max lay back down, closed his eyes and resumed napping.

Daisy's knees crumbled and she collapsed onto her chest. Many dogs sobbed while others loudly wailed. Buddy thrust his paw through the crate and thrashed at the latch. Jillian bit the crate's metal bars. Teddy twirled in tight circles, as did several other Greyhounds.

Now Daisy knew why Irving was trying hard to persuade her to escape. She realized he must have known about dogs that were taken away but wanted to keep the ugly truth from her. At that moment, Daisy decided she would escape. She made up her mind to do everything Irving said because she knew that her life was over if she stayed at the track.

Win or die. Max's words echoed in Daisy's head. *Win or die. Win or die.*

Chapter Six

Later that morning, when all the Greyhounds were let out into the exercise yard, Daisy and Irving's eyes met. They sprinted toward each other and both skidded to a stop inches apart.

"I need to get out!" Daisy paced back and forth as tears trickled down her snout. "Poor Dalton didn't know last night would be his last. I can't spend another night here. I thought that man was coming for me."

"Me too. My heart still hasn't stopped pounding."

"I can't wait."

"I know, I know. We'll escape after tonight's race."

"Not then, let's do it now."

"No, we can't."

"Show me where we can jump over. Let's go find a new home now. There's one out there, I just know it."

"Lower your voice." Irving glanced around. "If they notice us missing before the race, they might send out the—"

"So that's it! That's why you didn't want to tell me too much about the Rottweilers before. They would come after us right away?"

"But if we get out *after* the race, then they may not notice us missing for a while. We'll be way ahead."

Daisy gazed beyond the racetrack buildings. Massive tree limbs swayed in distant winds. "What happens if those Rottweilers catch us out there?"

"That *must* be avoided at all costs."

"I'll risk having those Rottweilers come after me. I'm sure I can outrun them."

Irving gazed at the border fence without saying anything for a moment. Daisy turned and also stared at the fence.

"I need to tell you a story," Irving said, not taking his eyes off the fence.

Daisy glanced back at him. "Another story? How many secret stories do you have?"

"This is what gave me the idea to get Everett to escape."

"Tell me. I've got nothing to lose now."

"About three years ago, a Greyhound from our kennel leaped over the border fence in broad daylight."

"So that's how you knew it could work—I mean with Everett?"

"Exactly. Otherwise I would've assumed it was impossible."

"Were they going to get rid of him?"

"No. Vernon was real fast. But he was always saying how much he hated it here. He constantly complained about the boring routine, the drab food, and...well, you know the rest."

A worker blew the whistle and the Greyhounds rushed toward the kennel to eat their breakfast. Daisy and Irving turned and shuffled behind.

"Then one afternoon," Irving continued, "we watched Vernon sprint across the yard like he didn't care who saw him. He scrambled over the fence without much difficulty."

"Wow!" Daisy said. "Then he must've found a home too."

Irving looked at Daisy and shook his head. "We saw some men from the track bring Vernon back when we were getting ready for that evening's race. The Rottweilers were with them. Vernon was howling and whining like I'd never seen any dog howl or whine. After that day, no one saw Vernon again."

Daisy looked blankly at Irving as if the last drop of her hope—what little she had—vanished.

"We'll need to be far away before they realize we're gone," Irving said.

Daisy lowered her head and nodded. Irving, seeing her deep sadness, came next to her and caressed her neck with his nose. Daisy then rubbed her head against Irving's cheek.

That evening, many of the dogs hung their heads in sorrow as they walked from their crates to the racetrack. There were several races as usual and Daisy's group was the evening's second.

Before the race began, the track workers paraded the dogs in front of the spectators in typical fashion. A new dog joined Daisy's group to replace Dalton. Spencer was at the track for only a couple of weeks but had already shown that he was very fast.

Tommy walked behind Spencer.

"Hey," Tommy said. "They took away the dog you replaced because he was too slow. Better keep up with me."

Spencer turned around and snarled. "Yeah, muscle head? You'll have enough trouble keeping up with me."

As the two dogs argued, Irving pulled his assigned track worker and came alongside Daisy. He leaned close to her.

"You'll need a lot of energy later. Don't try to run as hard tonight."

"I know, I was thinking the same thing. All afternoon, I've been wondering if I should even fake getting hurt out there so that I wouldn't have to use any energy because—"

"No, don't do that!"

"Why not?" Daisy's forehead wrinkled.

"Because they'll get you even before the race is over. They'll examine you for anything wrong. If they think you don't want to race anymore, you wouldn't stay here."

"So, I guess this is my last race." Daisy's shoulders sagged. "It didn't hit me until now but tonight I'm actually running my last race. If I make it over the fence then I'm free. If I don't, well, you know they wouldn't keep me here anymore—not after trying to escape."

"Escape?" A voice came from behind them.

Daisy and Irving traded shocking glances. They whipped their heads around and saw Milady glaring at them.

"I heard it all, Princess."

"Milady," Irving said with a bit of a stutter in his voice. "We didn't mean—"

"You're planning to escape." Milady drew closer and glared into Daisy's eyes.

Daisy backed up a couple steps. "We are...I mean, we aren't...Irving really meant that..."

Milady's track worker pulled her forward while Irving clenched his teeth. Then Milady turned back.

"You're taking me with you."

Daisy scowled at Milady. "Oh, won't your dear Tommy miss you?"

Irving jumped around Daisy and came face to face with Milady. "No way. You're not in it."

"Well, well." Milady sneered at Irving. "If I don't go, you don't go. I'll blab your secret all over the track."

Irving took a deep breath and didn't speak for several seconds. "Okay. I'll tell you everything after the race."

Daisy got into Irving's face. "Are you insane," she hissed. "She'll ruin it."

The track worker snapped Irving's leash and pulled him away. Just before he left Daisy's side, Irving thrust his snout into her ear. "Don't be so sure."

At the starting boxes, Tommy and Casey appeared to be chummy with each other. Milady shot Tommy a furious look as all the dogs scooted toward their slots. Tommy looked over his shoulder to make sure Milady didn't hear him. He bent his head towards Casey's ear.

"I've never seen a girl more beautiful than you," he said sweetly, giving her a wink.

Casey blinked her eyes and a happy smile appeared on her face. She trotted toward her starting box, still glancing back and smiling at him. Tommy, again, looked to see where Milady was, and then headed to his box too.

Daisy, who overheard the entire conversation, stood with her mouth hanging open. *So, now he likes Casey? That's a quick change!* Daisy shook her head in disbelief and amazement at Casey and Milady. *How could you two be so gullible over this tomcat?*

Milady caught Daisy's look just before all the dogs scooted into their boxes. "I guess beating you tonight will be easier than ever," she said. "After all, you wouldn't want to use all your energy."

"Ha, I still have one more chance to crush you!"

Then from one end of the starting boxes, Irving called out, "No, Daisy, remember—"

But before he could remind Daisy to conserve her energy, the buzzer went off and the gates flew open. The Greyhounds bolted from the boxes with a whoosh and blurred past the spectators. Muscle and sinew pounded the earth. They were bunched closely through the first and second turns. Surprisingly, Daisy was second and gaining on Tommy, who was in first place.

Irving also sped up, but he had a hard time reaching Daisy to get his message to her.

"Slow down! Slow down!"

But Daisy raced even faster. She came alongside Tommy and, for a fraction of a second, was in first place. Tommy made several quick glances at her in total disbelief. Then Spencer sprinted up and squeezed past Daisy. Tommy also regained his concentration and plowed by her, followed by all the other dogs.

Daisy struggled her hardest but rapidly fell to the back. The hounds banked the fourth and final turn. The finish line neared. Tommy thrust out his nose but Spencer's muzzle crossed the line just a whisker ahead of Tommy's. Irving followed a second later.

Daisy halted when she was inches from finish line. With her chest heaving, she glanced to her side at the white post that marked the end of the race. She knew it would be her last time to go across the line. Escape or no escape, she had failed to complete the race, which was one of the worst violations in dog racing.

While Daisy stood on the track, straddling the finish line, a track worker took off her muzzle and racing blanket just like he did with the other dogs that were panting hard after the exhausting race. Daisy was catching her breath when she noticed Tommy stepping over to Milady.

"I've never seen a girl more beautiful than you." He winked at her. "And faster, too."

"And I've just seen a dog who's faster than you." Milady stuck her nose in the air and marched away, winking to Spencer at the same time.

Daisy froze in disbelief at what she had just witnessed but her thoughts were interrupted when Irving sprinted up to her.

"Are you crazy?" Irving stomped his paw. "What was that speeding up all about?"

Daisy closed her eyes. Irving turned and looked at the border fence.

"Rats! You better have some strength left. Let's go."

Daisy and Irving plodded toward the fence in awkward silence. But they didn't get far before they heard a familiar voice from behind.

"So, what's the plan? Better tell me, or I'm gonna start barking."

Daisy and Irving whipped their heads around and saw Milady grinning at them.

"Okay, Milady." Irving signaled with his nose. "First we have to hide over there. C'mon, quickly."

Daisy watched in confusion as Irving loped off. Milady followed on his heels. Irving led Milady behind an old wooden box, just large enough to conceal her.

"I'll be right back. Be quiet and make sure no one sees you."

Milady nodded as Irving ran back to Daisy.

Meanwhile, alongside the kennel, Willie squatted next to a dog crate. He wore a welding mask as he fused broken metal bars with a torch.

Irving skidded to a stop next to Daisy. "Milady might be a bit late," he said, winking. "Let's get going. That man's back is facing us and the other track workers will be getting the next race ready."

Daisy glanced over to Willie. Sure enough, Willie was in his own world as he fumbled with the welding torch.

"Irving, how come you never escaped? You could've joined Everett a long time ago."

"I've thought about it a lot since he escaped."

"But it seems you could've gotten out of here anytime you wanted."

"Actually, I was seriously thinking of escaping three months ago, but then—"

"Hey, that's about when I came here. Boy, am I glad you—" Daisy's eyes became mesmerized as she absorbed what she had just begun to suspect—that

Irving hadn't escaped after she arrived at the track because of her. She quickly changed the subject.

"Do you think we can find a nice home like Everett did?" Daisy asked.

Irving tenderly gazed into her eyes. "We'll find a great home with people who'll love us and care for us for the rest of our lives. I promise."

"I hope so, because I'm tired of this racing and these crates... But most of all, I'm tired of being afraid."

Irving nodded. Then he suddenly became fidgety. "Okay, gotta do it now. Leap over it, just how I told you and then I'll follow. Wait for me in the trees."

Irving leaned over and kissed Daisy on the side of her nose. She gave him a stunned look.

"Irving?"

"No matter what happens, just know I love you. Now go!"

Daisy took a few steps but doubt quickly engulfed her face.

"I can't. It's too high."

"You can. Hurry!"

"I'm so scared."

"I wish I could take the leap for both of us, but I can't. It's up to you."

Daisy stared at the fence, which seemed even higher the closer she came to it.

Suddenly, a track worker blew a whistle to call the dogs into the kennel. The cool-off time was over. Daisy seemed paralyzed with fear and wouldn't budge. Irving then gave her a hard nudge against her back leg with his paw. Daisy exploded toward the fence, leaving a cloud of dust hanging in the air where the Greyhound had stood a second before.

Chapter Seven

Daisy darted across the hard earth toward the fence. Dirt kicked up behind her. When she was a few feet away, she launched herself as high as her remaining power would let her. She stretched her forelimbs and extended her toes. The attempt wasn't enough—she missed by two feet. The fatigued Greyhound crashed against the fence and tumbled onto the ground.

Irving gasped. All the dogs heading to the kennel whirled their heads when they heard the thud.

Willie looked over. He pulled off the mask and tossed the welding torch onto the table.

"What's going on over there?" He whipped out a leash and collar from his back pocket.

As Willie charged toward Daisy, he bumped the table. The torch rolled to the edge. It hesitated for a second and then plummeted to the ground. It landed in a pile of oily rags and smoldered. A yellow flame leaped up.

Milady had also heard the thud against the fence. She poked her nose around the corner of the box.

"Oh, you nasty dogs! You tricked me."

Irving ran to the fence and squatted down. "Try again. Use my back."

Daisy struggled to her feet. She rapidly blinked her eyes and shook her head.

"Now!" Irving pointed his nose at Willie. "He's right behind you."

Daisy dashed away just as Willie reached for her. She ran in a circle, getting enough speed.

"You ain't going anywhere," Willie yelled as he raced after her.

Daisy hopped onto Irving's back. At the exact same time that she did, he erupted to his feet and pushed her up. This time, Daisy was able to get a hold of the top of the fence. While her front legs hung over, she clawed at the wood with her hind legs. Willie reached the fence and Irving leaped aside. Willie then grabbed Daisy's hind legs and began to pull her down.

"Irving! Help me."

Irving growled at Willie and showed his teeth. Willie lifted his boot and kicked him away.

"Get back to the kennel. Now!"

Irving slipped to his knees as he absorbed the impact of Willie's foot. Willie then pulled harder on

Daisy and she started to lose her grip. Irving lifted his chin and watched helplessly as Daisy let out an agonizing whine. A searing pain blazed through her body. Saliva poured from her mouth and dripped into the weeds below.

"Please, Irving, where are you?" Daisy twisted her head and looked down at Irving. He was in a stupor and seemed unable to stand back up.

"You ain't getting away from me," Willie shrieked. "Never."

Daisy slipped further. The veins and tendons in her legs seemed like they were about to split wide open.

"Irving, for Priscilla's sake!"

Irving raised his head. His eyes bulged and he sprang up with a surge of power. "I'm coming! Hold on!"

Irving rushed over and sank his teeth into Willie's backside.

"Ouch! Why you—" Willie released his grip on Daisy's legs and fell to one knee. Daisy then inched her way back up the fence.

Willie got to his feet but Irving knocked him down with his front paws. Willie bounced back up and faced Irving in a wrestler's stance. Irving darted past Willie and came underneath Daisy. He stood on his hind legs and leaned against the fence.

"Push off my head," Irving shouted. "Quickly."

Daisy's back legs touched Irving's head. Willie then grabbed Irving around his chest and swung him away. Irving dropped to the ground and out of Willie's grasp. Willie immediately lost his balance. He staggered and then fell against the fence, all the while remaining on his feet.

Daisy's feet continued to feel for Irving's head. Instead, her paws located Willie's forehead. She pushed against it and climbed the rest of the way to the top. But her toenails tore into Willie's skin.

"Arrrrgggg!" Blood trickled into his eyes.

Meanwhile, Daisy teetered on top of the fence. After Willie wiped his face with his shirt, he looked up at Daisy. She stared back. Willie grinned and moved his hand up. Daisy froze as his hand came closer—and closer. She turned and glanced down onto the other side of the fence. She was a long ways off the ground. But just as Willie took a swipe at her dangling tail, Daisy let herself fall to the other side.

Willie slammed his palm against the fence and then twirled around. He reached down and grabbed Irving by the skin on the back of his neck. Then he put the collar on and attached the leash.

"Oh, don't you worry. I'll get your friend back. None of my dogs gets away from me. None!"

Meanwhile, all the dogs gathered and watched the scene from a distance.

"I can't believe it!" Porter looked over at the fence. "I didn't think a dog could get over that."

"She's gonna get it now." Spencer wagged his head. "So, that was their plan. I knew something was up when Irving told her to slow down."

Willie led Irving to the kennel as the dog frantically resisted, but the grip remained firm. Irving turned his head toward the fence with a devastated look.

Two track workers, Rick and Dave, ran up to Willie.

"We got a runaway?" Rick asked.

"That dog won't be too far." Willie gripped the leash tighter. "Gotta capture her before nightfall."

"We'll get her." Dave nodded with confidence. "Probably ran under a bush or something."

"Mr. McKenzie's gonna now want to get rid of her," Rick said.

Willie pulled Irving forward. "Right on schedule. She was gonna be shipped out tomorrow morning."

"What happened to you?" Dave asked, gawking at Willie's forehead. "That's a nasty cut."

"That monster! She dug her grimy claws into me. When we get her back I'm going to—"

"Wait." Rick stuck his nose into the air. "What's that smell?"

As the three came into view of the kennel, they stopped in shock. Fiery tongues licked the outside kennel wall. Willie released his grip on Irving's leash and whipped out a cell phone.

Rick ran toward the kennel. "Hey, there's a bunch of dogs still in there!"

Chapter Eight

Daisy crashed through the dimly lit underbrush without looking back. Saplings whipped at her legs. Her paws stumbled upon endless branches and twigs as enormous maples and oaks stretched their black arms over her. A couple of owls took off from their perches, startled by the oncoming bolt of flesh through the thickets.

Daisy veered into the more open areas of the forest. Five minutes later, she scurried behind a large, rotting log and collapsed. Her chest quaked uncontrollably in the warm evening air. She tried not to breathe too loudly, but her lungs wouldn't obey. Lying on the forest floor, Daisy listened for dogs barking and men yelling. She knew that if the Rottweilers picked up her trail and found her, there would be nothing she could do to escape or fend them off. They would tear her to pieces.

"Irving," she whispered, "c'mon, c'mon."

Back at the kennel, smoke poured out of the building's ventilation screens while dogs yelped and barked from inside. The track workers bolted through the doorway where they found the dogs coughing and wheezing in the thickening smoke.

The Greyhounds collided with each other as they struggled to find their way out of the building. Many of them were bumping into walls and crates as the men tried to grab them by the collars and get them out. Some resisted, not knowing that the men were trying to save their lives.

Suddenly, the sprinklers in the ceiling came on and streams of water burst out of tiny nozzles. The floor became a slippery brew of water and dog saliva. People and canines tripped and stumbled over each other. Several dogs crawled back into their crates as if that would be the safest place to hide.

When the track workers couldn't endure the smoke any longer, they felt their way toward the exit. Some of the dogs still had leashes on with no one to pull them to safety.

Irving watched the three track workers stagger outside, each one gasping for air. By this time, more track workers had run over, but none dared to go inside. Without wasting a second, Irving torpedoed into the kennel. Tommy and Spencer exchanged quick glances and then followed. Milady and Casey stood outside and looked on with horror.

Irving burst back through the doorway, lugging a dog by its collar. Tommy and Spencer also came out, leading two more dogs. The three Greyhounds dashed back inside as other dogs rushed out to escape the burning kennel.

The pounding inside Daisy's chest softened. Lifting her head, she angled her ears and listened for anyone approaching. But the only sound was the music from an army of mosquitoes humming around her head. Then a distant siren cut through the night air. Daisy stood with her ears straight up and pondered the bizarre, far-away sound.

Three fire trucks, with sirens blaring, turned onto the track property. By now, the flames had crawled all the way to the kennel roof. The fire trucks screeched to a stop and firemen spilled out. They scattered across the parking lot, pulling long hoses behind. At the same time, three blue vans exited the parking lot along with the last of the spectators.

Daisy emerged from the woods and stood in the high grass. Her jaw dropped. Much of track area was filled with black smoke. She could see golden flames dancing atop the kennel.

"Oh, no!" Daisy scrambled up a nearby hill to get a better view. "What's happening there? Where are the dogs?"

From the hill, Daisy wept as she watched arching streams of foamy liquid fall upon the building. She turned her face away from the blackened shell when the saturated wood emitted a ghastly hissing noise. The air reeked of charred lumber. The smoke worsened and for a moment Daisy lost sight of the kennel.

By now, the sun had long disappeared, replaced by the fire trucks' headlights and the orange glow from the burning building.

A thick haze of smoke drifted over Daisy. She felt nauseous. Knowing that there was nothing she could do, she turned back toward the trees. Then she heard screaming and yelling. She wheeled her head around. Several firemen dropped their axes and hoses and scrambled away from the kennel. With her mouth gaping, Daisy watched the kennel walls fall outward. The roof quickly followed, collapsing into a crimson, smoldering heap. Sparks burst into the night sky like a million fireflies racing toward the moon. Only the gray cinder block foundation remained.

For several minutes, the horror of seeing her former home disintegrate didn't allow Daisy to budge. But the smoke engulfed the woods and she was forced to retreat deeper into the trees. Once she got far enough to breathe without inhaling mouthfuls of smoke, she let her body crumple onto the ground.

"Oh, Irving," Daisy moaned. "What am I going to do without you?"

Sprawled on the forest floor, Daisy relived the scene of the fire over and over. The sight of the kennel crashing into a pile of twisted, blazing timber kept flashing in front of her eyes. For several hours, she stared into the blackness of the forest. Sleep was fleeting, but as the strain from the race and the escape caught up with her, Daisy eventually dozed off.

Chapter Nine

The next morning, Willie opened the door to the racetrack office. He took a deep breath as he softly closed the door behind him. A middle-aged man had his back to him.

"I need to talk to you, Mr. McKenzie. Look, I know—"

"You got your notice. You're fired," Mr. McKenzie said as he sorted through paperwork in a filing cabinet.

"Please?" Willie released a groan.

Mr. McKenzie turned around. "It's my final word. Look, I'm busy."

"Won't fire insurance cover everything?"

"Thank goodness."

"I need this job." Willie's voice got more desperate.

Mr. McKenzie's face became red. "And I needed you to be responsible. I could've lost all those dogs, instead of the one that ran off."

Willie fell to his knees and extended his hands. "Please! Give me another chance."

"No, I'm sorry." Mr. McKenzie turned back to the filing cabinet. "Besides, I don't like what I've heard about the way you treat the dogs. If you got some kind of thing about having power over these animals, then you're in the wrong profession."

Willie sprang up, barged out of the office and slammed the door. He didn't get more than ten feet when Dave ran up to him.

"Any luck?" he asked.

"No, but I'll change his mind."

"How you gonna do that?"

Willie glanced over to the green fence, the very spot where Daisy went over the evening before. "When I bring that dog back, then he'll know I'm responsible."

"I thought they were gonna get rid of her anyway."

"Doesn't matter. She was my dog and none of my dogs ever stick it to me like that." Willie brushed Dave aside and marched off.

Daisy woke up that morning with a heavy heart. Hoping that the kennel fire was simply the worst nightmare of her life, she headed back to the racetrack to make sure. As she stood in the tall grass at the edge of the woods, well hidden from view, a tear dribbled down her snout—she had not been dreaming.

Most of the smoke had cleared but several plumes of blue-gray haze rose from the ashes. While she watched several people rummage among the ruins, Daisy tried to imagine what could have happened to the other Greyhounds.

Maybe I'll hear some of the dogs, she thought. *Maybe I'll even see Irving.*

A couple of hours later, when dump trucks arrived to haul away the scorched timber, Daisy guessed her kennel mates were no longer at the track. *They must've gotten out of the fire, but what if they didn't?* She wouldn't consider the worst—for now. She wandered back into the trees, desperately wondering what she should do next.

A while later, Daisy stepped out of the woods and into a huge field that smelled of dry hay and horse manure. She looked to her left and saw horses grazing. Then she glanced further around and, to her amazement, she could see the racetrack lights rising above the tree line in the distance. In front of her stood a red farmhouse with white trim and shutters. But it wasn't more than a few seconds before a twig snapped. Her ears pricked up and she whirled her head to the right. Standing under an oak tree just a few feet from her was the same Afghan Hound that she saw a few days before in the red Corvette.

"Who are you?" he asked. "What are you doing on my farm?"

Daisy stared at his silky hair that glistened in the sunlight and waved in the gentle breeze. His face had the same shape as a Greyhound's, except a little smaller. His snout was much darker too.

"You lost?" The Afghan Hound walked from the shadows.

"Uh, I don't know. Where am... Hey, I saw you the other day."

"Then you're from over there." The Afghan Hound motioned with his long snout toward the track grounds.

"There was a fire—"

"I saw the smoke and lots of flashing lights. Heard a whole bunch of barking too."

Daisy stepped closer to the Afghan Hound. "The whole kennel burned down and it's tearing me apart not knowing what happened to the other dogs."

"Maybe they left in those vans that drove out of there. I was with my owner by the roadside as we watch the commotion. What a horrible sight it was—never seen anything like it in my life."

Daisy suddenly appeared gloomy. "I'd never be able to find them if they got out. I was supposed to find a new home with Irving, but now...I guess I'll have to do it by myself."

"By yourself? Out there? Are you nuts? You have to be careful. Don't let them get you."

"Who?" Daisy returned a puzzled look.

"The dogcatchers, of course. They'll think you're a stray."

"A what?"

"C'mon. Everyone knows what a stray is. It's a dog that has no home."

"But I'll find a home soon."

"Them dogcatchers will chase you down and take you to that awful place."

Daisy looked even more confused.

The Afghan Hound stared at Daisy as if she was the only dog in the world that didn't know what happened to stray dogs.

"You know, the dog pound," the Afghan Hound said. "Most dogs that are caught are never seen again."

"Maybe that's where they take all the Greyhounds, like Jasper and Dalton."

"I've heard it's a terrible place filled with dirty and smelly street dogs that always lived outside."

Daisy shook her head. "Seems like it would be worse than going back to the track."

"I'm telling you, avoid them at all costs."

Daisy scanned the field. "Then where can I go? I need to get as far from the track as possible before they find me."

The Afghan Hound gestured with his snout, this time pointing to the road that curved around the field. "Follow that road. There's a town down there with lots of houses. Maybe someone there will want you. Better find a home soon. Cold weather's coming."

Daisy stared in the same direction and noticed how the road snaked far into the distance. She somberly thanked the Afghan Hound for his help and scampered off toward the town.

Chapter Ten

Three weeks later, on a chilly October morning, Daisy squeezed from underneath a Ford pick-up truck that had four flat tires—the same vehicle where she had spent every cramped night since arriving at the town. She was dirtier and thinner but still had a lot of determination to find a new home. And, for sure, Cedartown had many homes.

Much of Daisy's time had been spent roving along store-lined streets, exploring residential neighborhoods or wandering around parking lots. She hoped someone—anyone—would see her and realize she needed a real home. But she wouldn't let her guard down. The dogcatchers were out there ready to grab her or do whatever it is dogcatchers do to homeless dogs. But Daisy knew she wasn't homeless—at least not for long. Besides, she had her pick-up truck.

During her search for a home, Daisy had seen many dogs peering out at her from behind windows or screen doors. Many were strange-looking dogs—breeds she had never seen before. Some were short with squatty legs. Others were round with tiny crumpled noses. But the most bizarre dog she saw was one with frizzy black fur around its face, ankles, and the tip of its tail while the rest of its body was almost hairless. Dachshunds, Bulldogs, and Poodles were only a small part of the new world that Daisy had encountered.

Daisy also had seen children drawing with chalk on driveways or bicycling along the sidewalks. She was tempted to lope over to them but was apprehensive, not knowing whether they would be scared of her—or her of them.

To find food, Daisy would get up on her hind legs and dip her snout into the numerous garbage cans standing along the street. But she was usually rewarded with a mouthful of banana peels or plastic wrappers. Once, she found a half-eaten hamburger buried under a pile of yellow leaves. She gobbled it up—the best meal she had since escaping from the track. But she was hungry most of the time and would usually go to sleep with a growling stomach.

But this particular day started off great. The smell of raw meat tickled her nostrils, causing her stomach to rumble like never before. She paused on the sidewalk and stretched her muzzle high into the air to locate where the smell was coming from. Her nose quickly guided her to a six-foot high wall of green sculptured shrubs.

She trotted up to the hedge, darted her eyes around its roots, and hoped that someone had accidentally dropped a bag of meat. Seeing nothing, but finding the smell getting stronger, Daisy guessed that the meat was either in the bushes or somewhere on the other side.

The hungry canine pressed her nose through the hedge. Saliva dribbled down the leafless twigs inside. Daisy closed her eyes and gingerly pushed her nose through the tangled maze of prickly branches. Her head and neck were soon swallowed up. Just as her snout came to the opposite side, she heard muffled voices. She peered into a courtyard and made out several dogs standing in a circle. In the middle of the group lay a huge steak, partially wrapped with brown butcher's paper.

"Next time, I want better cooperation between you two," a heavy voice bellowed. "You didn't fool anyone with that horrible act. We were lucky to get what we did. Maybe I'll eat this steak myself."

Daisy peeked over a branch to better see the owner of the voice. She almost gasped out loud. It was a Rottweiler! A huge, mean-looking, black Rottweiler—even larger than the ones the track workers owned.

"But Samson," a brown, long-haired mutt said, nodding at a black mutt whose head was half white, being divided exactly in the middle from between his ears to the tip of his snout. "Domino is never doing as he should. That's why it doesn't look real."

"Don't listen to him," Domino said. "Harley hesitates when I'm about to fight back. That's why I don't attack him. He needs to resist me better."

Samson stepped between the two mutts. "If you don't cooperate next time, then I'll find two others to take your place."

"You heard him," piped in a red-chestnut Chihuahua whom Daisy just noticed standing under Samson's chest. He had runaway from his owner because he had grown tired of being kept alone inside an apartment all day. He also hated to wear the little blue vest when going for walks. Enough was enough. "Get your act together or find another gang. We can always find a couple other tomatoes."

"Hold on, Georgie," a German Shepherd said. He had joined the group after his owner abandoned him a month before. But he didn't mind. He would have taken off eventually. Being tied up with a chain all day and walking in circles around a tree just wasn't his thing. He had stood in silence until a strange odor overtook the aroma of the streak. "Anyone else get a whiff of that?" he asked.

"Of what?" the two mutts asked in unison.

"Stop arguing and stick your noses into the air," Samson said. "Trapper noticed something, and now I smell it too."

"It's coming from these bushes." Harley nodded in Daisy's direction.

"Look at that!" Georgie's ruby eyes glared at the wall of green needles. The other four focused on the spot where his paw was pointing.

"It's moving. What is it?" Domino watched the black, wet nostrils wiggle in the open air of the courtyard.

"I think it's another dog," Samson said. "It's gotta be a spy!"

Knowing she had been seen, Daisy yanked her nose back through the hedge.

Samson waved a paw. "Let's go get 'em!"

The dogs ran out of the courtyard, three went to the left, two to the right. They surrounded Daisy just as she pulled her head out of the bushes.

"Excuse me," Samson said, forcing a gentle, almost musical tone into his voice that was obviously phony. "Are we disturbing you?"

"Oh, no," Daisy replied, trying to smile. "You're—"

Samson suddenly growled and shoved his nose into Daisy's cheek. "What do you think you're going to find?" His hot breath forced her to turn her head away. She swallowed hard.

"Who sent you?" Georgie demanded as his ears flared straight up off his tiny skull. "What did you hear?"

"I'm...I mean...I was really hungry." Daisy could barely find her voice. "I was just looking for food. I smelled meat."

"You were spying on us." Samson's narrowed his eyes and his voice became a hiss. "We've never seen you around here before. Come with us."

The dogs boxed in Daisy and forced her around the hedges and into the courtyard. She hesitated to run away. She assumed that the five knew the neighborhood well, which would make it pointless to try and flee.

"Who are you?" Harley asked with a scowl.

"Yeah, what were you doing around here?" Domino pressed his face, with nostrils flaring, into Daisy's forehead. "What's your name?"

"Uh...I'm Daisy." A shiver rattled down her spine. "I didn't mean to cause any trouble. I get so hungry in the mornings."

Samson snarled at the two mutts for jumping in ahead of him. "I'll take over from here, if you two don't mind." Then he turned to Daisy. "Don't you get fed? Where's your home then?"

"I don't have a home but I'm looking for one. The place I lived was burned down a while ago."

Samson looked at Daisy's trembling legs and noticed how muscular they were. His eyes widened and a smile slipped across his face.

"Can you ran fast?" he asked.

"Well...yeah...I used to race and—"

"Great. Why don't you join us?"

"Why don't we just tear her apart and get it over with?" Georgie made himself look like he was ready to lunge at Daisy as he stood underneath Samson's belly.

"Shut up! Who's the boss here?" Samson bowed his head and looked at Georgie. "I've got a plan," he whispered.

He turned back to Daisy. "I'll give you this meat. But you'll do something for me."

Daisy gazed at the steak as saliva dripped from her open mouth. Samson swatted the steak and it landed on top of her paws.

"Anything you want." Daisy looked hypnotized.

Meanwhile, the four other dogs gathered several feet away. Each furled their brow as they spoke in hushed voices.

"What's he doing?" Georgie hissed and glanced over his shoulder at Samson.

"He's giving away our breakfast," Harley whispered.

"He doesn't even know who she is," Domino said, being even more careful not to let Samson hear.

Daisy dug her teeth into the steak as Samson revealed his gang's purpose.

"None of us have a home. We hafta to work hard together to survive. We try to have several operations each week and we have to come up with different ideas to snatch food from people, from stores, from anywhere. It takes a real lot of planning. When we take food, we divide it between ourselves. We ripped that steak out of someone's hands this morning. We could have gotten more if those two—"

"Isn't she going to save some for us?" Harley asked as the four dogs returned and formed a semi-circle around Daisy and Samson.

"You barely earned it," Samson snapped back. "Now keep quiet." Turning back to Daisy, he continued. "We mostly get food by grabbing bags out of people's hands as they walk from a grocery store. We got this idea one day when we noticed another dog grabbing a bag of food from some kid."

"It was my idea, I saw him do it." Domino puffed up his chest.

"Who cares? What would you do with that idea by yourself, dummy?" Georgie stepped from under Samson and glared at Domino, who raised his paw as if he was going to belt Georgie. Just in case, the tiny Chihuahua slipped back underneath Samson's chest. But Georgie really had no fear of other dogs—as long as Samson was there.

"Both of you keep quiet." Samson dipped his neck and shivered while Georgie's ears tickled his belly. "Get out from there and let me talk with her."

Daisy swallowed another piece of meat. "How long have you been doing this?"

"Those two for a year. The little guy about six months, and Trapper just joined."

"Are there any more of you?" Daisy asked, spitting out a bone.

"Others were with us in the past but they were all picked up. Never heard from them again."

"They were stupid for getting caught," Georgie said. "They deserved to rot in the dog pound."

"The dog pound?" Daisy's ears perked up and she stopped chewing. "There's one around here?"

"They've been on to us recently," Samson said. "There's this one dogcatcher that's been around a couple weeks who seems to come just when we want to steal something. Nasty looking guy."

"How come you don't get caught?"

"It's not easy anymore because we're getting recognized on the streets. People kick us or yell at us when we get near to them. That's why we need you to help us. We'll split the reward with you. These streets will be your home."

Daisy looked hard into Samson's eyes. "But I thought a home was—"

"Forget about the home you're looking for. We've got a great place in some old warehouse, if you don't mind a few rats running around."

"You all live in a house with rats?"

"A house? Ha!" Samson shook his head and released a fake chuckle. "I once lived in a house in this city. Never again! Also, by the time you'd ever find a home, you'd freeze to death. No, you'll be staying with us."

"Well, I'm going to live in a house—a nice house. Besides, I'm not going to steal from anyone."

Daisy turned and started to walk away but the five dogs immediately boxed her in. Samson stepped forward.

"I guess you don't understand," he said, using his phony, soft voice. "You don't have a choice."

Chapter Eleven

During the rest of that morning and into the afternoon, the gang told Daisy about all the different methods to steal food from people. The best way would require all five dogs. Three would be directly engaged with the steal while two others would watch for police or the dogcatchers. The three involved in the theft would approach a person holding a bag that might have meat in it. Two dogs would stage a fight on one side of the person while the other dog would sneak up, grab the bag and then take off. Most of the time, the person didn't know what happened until it was too late.

An operation was planned for later that day. Daisy was told to be the bag-snatcher since she was the fastest. She also didn't look like a stray dog as much.

Around four o'clock, the dogs got together in an alley near the downtown. People were already hustling from their offices and shops. Late afternoon was the best time to steal because those involved with the theft could blend in with the crowds until they were ready to stage their fight.

From behind a trashcan, at the alley entrance, the dogs watched people stream by. Each dog smelled the air to detect if anyone carried a bag with meat.

"How 'bout that guy over there?" Domino suggested. "He's carrying something under his arm."

"Nah," Trapper said. "He's grasping it too close. Besides, I don't like the size of those boots he's wearing. Been kicked by boots like those. Not fun."

Daisy glanced at Samson while he scanned the sidewalk for a victim. Even though he was a huge, vicious-looking dog, she had begun to feel sorry for him.

"Samson, what did you mean when you said you'd never live in a house again in this city?"

Samson whipped his head around and faced Daisy with glowering eyes. It appeared that he was caught off guard with her question. Daisy then sensed that somehow bringing this up was probably not the wise thing to do.

"None of your business," Samson replied bluntly. "I hate homes and I don't want to talk about it."

Daisy looked at him searchingly, trying to dissect his thoughts. Realizing she would get nothing more out of him, she returned her gaze to the street. Samson did the same.

"Let's take that one." Samson pointed to an elegant-looking woman in a stylish dress, who had just exited a delicatessen with a white plastic bag.

The store owner waved to her as he stood in the doorway. "Have a nice afternoon, Mrs. Clark."

The woman smiled back and strolled in the direction of the dog gang. She was still several storefronts away when they all saw her open her black handbag.

"She just stuffed something into that bag," Georgie yapped.

"Daisy, go with Domino and Harley." Samson prodded her forward with his huge paw. "Remember, don't grab the bag until she reacts to the fight. When you grab it, run back to the courtyard."

"Hurry!" Georgie's voice became little more than a squeal. "She's getting closer."

All six poked their heads out of the alley.

"Don't forget," Samson said, shooting a threatening glare at Daisy, "me and Trapper are watching you. If you try to run off, we'll find you. We know the turf. Do yourself a favor and do as I say. Maybe we'll snag some lamb."

Mrs. Clark passed the dogs without noticing the gang hidden in the shadows.

"Now, get going," Samson said. "Be quick about it but be careful. Keep half an eye out for that dogcatcher."

The three left the alley. The sidewalks were quickly filling up with workers rushing to get home or to catch a bus. Domino and Harley went ahead of Daisy. She quietly followed the two mutts from several yards behind.

Domino and Harley sneaked up beside Mrs. Clark and began to growl and hiss at each other. She glanced down for a moment, but didn't take any further interest. She fixed her eyes straight ahead and continued to walk. The dogs barked more ferociously and flattened their ears on their heads. Mrs. Clark looked down again, this time longer.

The fight began. The two actor-warriors gnashed at each other's snouts, being careful only to get them wet. They had become so good at the charade that they could make their mouths foam with saliva any time they wanted. They whirled around and took fake bites at each other's fur. At this point, Mrs. Clark, as well as several other pedestrians, paused to watch. Mrs. Clark backed up several feet toward Daisy, giving the two fighters more room. Several others did the same. Some people shrieked, worried that the two dogs would kill each other.

Mrs. Clark retreated even more until she was almost in Daisy's face. The Greyhound's long muzzle was inches from the black handbag. She snatched the bag and gently pulled the straps off the woman's shoulder. Mrs. Clark never felt a thing. Then Daisy turned and sprinted back toward the alley.

From there, Samson, Georgie and Trapper saw Daisy make the steal.

"She got it!" Trapper jumped two feet in the air.

"To the courtyard we go." Samson's face beamed with delight.

"I'm gonna give her a big kiss," Georgie cried out. "But first I'll eat."

The three bolted over to the courtyard to meet Daisy there.

Domino and Harley, also noticing that Daisy had taken the bag, brought their fight to Mrs. Clark's feet. They rolled on the ground, growling and barking at each other as Daisy disappeared into the crowd. Then Mrs. Clark reached to pull her handbag closer. Her face became a mask of confusion. She twirled her head and looked over her shoulder.

"My bag! My bag!" Mrs. Clark spun around, glancing every which way.

Domino and Harley jumped to their feet and chased each other toward the alley in a different direction than Daisy went, to create a diversion. At the same time, one of the spectators of the fight took out his cell phone and called the police. Another called animal control.

Chapter Twelve

When Daisy got far enough away, she stopped to catch her breath. She looked back up the street and realized no one had yet followed. Then she noticed her reflection in a clothing store window. She stared at herself with the handbag dangling from her mouth.

What have I done? Daisy slowly shook her head as a guilty look washed over her. She had never seen a full reflection of herself before. The only times she did see herself was in her water bowl and one time in the side-view mirror of the van that had brought her to the Blue Arrow Racing Park. Now, she only saw a simple thief in that store window—a thief who had given up her quest to find her dream home.

Daisy gazed far up the street. A group of people surrounded Mrs. Clark, who covered her face with her palms. Another woman put an arm around her shoulder.

Meanwhile, Samson, Georgie and Trapper were already sitting in the shade of the courtyard when Domino and Harley came panting into the hideaway.

"What took you two so long?" Samson sprang to his feet and snarled at the two mutts.

"Hey, needed a fire hydrant break." Harley shrugged and gave Samson an awkward look.

"Whew!" Domino shook his head and giggled. "Did you see how easily she grabbed that thing?"

"I never saw a dog take off so fast." Harley licked his chops. "We gotta do this every day."

"Then where is she?" Georgie asked. "If she's so fast, she should've gotten here already."

"Looks like you'll have to wait to give her that big kiss." Trapper snickered and gave Georgie a playful tap on his head.

Georgie shot back a scornful look.

"She would have been here by now," Harley said, finally catching his breath.

"Maybe she couldn't find her way?" Domino said.

"Let's give her five more minutes." Samson paced back and forth. "Then we'll go back out and find her. She had better be lost for her own good."

Five minutes later, the gang returned near to the crime scene and investigated from a distance.

Willie Sharp sat in the passenger side of a white van that had the words *'Cedartown Animal Control'* painted on its side. He was suited in a gray uniform, just like his new boss, Uncle Marty, who was the driver.

After getting fired from the racetrack, Willie had rushed to his uncle's house and begged him for a job. Although Marty had already hired someone, he gave in to Willie's pleadings and also hired him with the condition that he would treat the dogs well. Also, Willie would have to ride in the van with him since Marty was very overweight and needed someone to do the legwork in capturing most of the strays. Willie, of course, agreed, but he had other plans in mind—plans that involved recapturing a certain Greyhound that had gotten away from him weeks before.

Willie turned off a two-way radio and placed it back on the dashboard as the van motored along the highway.

"Just got a report that there was a bunch of stray dogs in the downtown on Pine Street, including a Greyhound. That's gotta be her for sure!"

"Who?" Marty asked.

Willie pointed to a scar on his forehead. "The one who left me this souvenir."

Marty shook his head without bothering to look at Willie. "You're still all obsessed with that hound? Forget about it. We've got enough strays to worry about."

"I lost my job at the track because of her. I lost even more than a job. I had power there and now I'm a nobody."

"You're lucky you only lost a job. You're even luckier you have this one. Good thing that fire was ruled an accident. The police could've blamed you."

"That dog's to blame. If she didn't escape—"

Marty stopped Willie with an upraised hand. "I said forget it. Besides, why do you have to be so mean to these dogs?"

Willie looked straight ahead with a scowl. Then a twisted smile developed on his face.

"None of my dogs ever get away from me," he mumbled under his breath. "I'll be top dog again."

The dog gang strutted up Pine Street, close to where Daisy made the steal.

"I think she's lost," Domino said. "She seemed like she enjoyed taking part."

Samson shook his head. "Something still bothers me. She was almost too willing to join us."

"She shouldn't have joined us before we knew if she could be one of us," Georgie piped in. "But who listens to me?"

Samson gave him a frown but said nothing.

"Maybe she was hungry and thought she had no choice?" Trapper reasoned.

"Well, she can't be too far." Samson glanced up and down the sidewalk. "Let's ask that dog over there. He was around the whole time. He could've seen where that scoundrel went."

A Foxhound was tied out in front of a café, waiting for his owner who had gone in a while before. Upon seeing the five strays, he immediately stood up and entered into a fighting stance.

"Relax, we just want to ask you a question," Samson said. "We're looking for a lost Greyhound. She was around here a little while ago. Have you seen her?"

"Why are you looking for her?"

"Her owner's been searching all over for her. He just got her and then she ran away a few hours ago. He's heartbroken and we're helping to find her."

"Yeah? You expect me to believe that? What did she look like then?"

"Skinny legs, brown and white fur," Georgie injected. "And a real long nose."

"And why should I tell you, even if I did see her?"

"Because you want to avoid trouble. Isn't that right?" Samson closed in on the Foxhound with a scowl on his face.

"Look, that dog means nothing to me," the Foxhound said, trembling. "I'll tell you."

Georgie came out from under Samson's chest and shoved a paw to an inch from the tip of the Foxhound's nose. "Smart move, now go ahead."

"A while ago...I saw a dog like that...maybe ten minutes ago." All five dogs' ears perked up. "She ran by me holding some black bag in her mouth."

"Which way?" Trapper asked.

"Toward the downtown." The Foxhound pointed with his paw.

All the dogs gazed toward the downtown.

"I think you mean she ran *away* from the downtown," Samson said, with an uneasy voice.

"No, it was definitely to the downtown."

The dogs gave each other troubling looks. Then they tripped over each other as they scrambled away from the café and toward where the Foxhound had pointed.

Chapter Thirteen

Daisy bashfully trotted up to Mrs. Clark and placed the handbag at her feet. A policeman stood next to her.

"Hey, my bag!" she cried out joyfully. "How'd this dog know that was *my* bag?"

The policeman bent down, picked up the handbag and gave it to the woman. "Amazing! Maybe she saw the guy who stole it and went and grabbed it back."

Nearby, the dog gang peered around a corner and watched in shock what was happening. When they saw what Daisy had done, it all hit them at once.

"Our food!" Domino wailed. "She gave it back."

"She played us for fools," Harley added. "She won't get away with this."

Georgie could hardly contain his rage as he danced on his toes. "She'll pay the price. Wait till I get hold of those skinny legs."

Samson gritted his teeth. "Then, as soon as she's alone, we'll get her."

Several witnesses to the dogfight stood in a group around the policeman, who was taking notes. Mrs. Clark leaned over and patted Daisy's head. Daisy gazed up into her eyes.

"What a good doggie," Mrs. Clark said. "Don't you have a home, girl? Want to come with me? You're so dirty so the first thing you'll need is a warm bath."

Daisy's tail sliced through the air as Mrs. Clark stroked Daisy's ears. Daisy closed her eyes and let herself drift into another world—a world she had dreamed about for a long time.

At that moment, the animal control van pulled alongside the curb. The squeak of the parking brake startled Daisy. She opened her eyes.

Willie rolled down the window and stuck out his head. "Hey, there some stray dogs around here?"

As soon as Willie saw Daisy, his mouth dropped and his eyes ballooned.

"Hey, lady!" He kicked open the cab door. "Hold that dog!"

Willie jumped onto the sidewalk and rushed toward Daisy. She broke from the crowd and scurried away.

Mrs. Clark stared at Willie with a furious look. "Now look what you've done. You've scared her away for good."

Willie watched Daisy barrel off and vanish into the nearest alley.

"Why do you care?" Willie glared back at Mrs. Clark. "That dog is a runaway. It's my job to get her—not yours."

"It's not your job to scare dogs half to death."

"Lady, just stay out of my business."

Willie trudged back to the van, pounded the door with his fist, and then got back in.

The gang dogs, who had been watching the entire ordeal, weren't so frustrated.

"Excellent, there she goes," Samson said. "Let's split up and find her before that dogcatcher does. Whoever finds her first, bark three times as loud as you can."

"Why are you so calm," Trapper asked. "She really stuck it to you."

The dogs watched Samson as his face washed over in anger. "If she thinks she's gonna find a home, she's got another thing coming."

Georgie grinned and looked up into Samson's furious eyes. "There's that inner rage I love so much."

The dogs split into three groups. Domino and Harley would search the alleys together, while Trapper and Georgie would explore the busier streets. Samson would go at it alone and look into the residential areas.

A few minutes later, Domino and Harley were probing under every piece of garbage as they waded through an alley littered with everything imaginable. They peered into crawl spaces or any other place a Greyhound might hide.

"She never should've joined us." Domino gobbled up a potato chip that had blown from the direction of a ventilation shaft.

Harley nodded. "She knows our best secret and now we have to dig though this filth. Samson and his stupid ideas."

A few blocks away, Trapper wandered with his nose plastered to the ground. Georgie walked under his chest.

"Stop getting underneath me." Trapper peered between his front legs.

"But that's the way me and Samson always do things," Georgie replied with a tone of pity in his voice.

"Your ears will tickle me to death."

"But what if some big, mean dog tries to chomp on me? How will I get protection?"

Trapper jutted out his chest. "I'm a big, mean dog. What if I decide to chomp on you?"

"You wouldn't harm a buddy, would ya? Our types have to stick together."

"Whatever." Trapper kept sniffing the ground. "Just go on searching."

Then they came to a sewer grate.

"Hey, you can see our reflections." Georgie pressed his face to the metal. "Boy, that's deep."

"She's not gonna be down there." Trapper didn't bother to glance down into the artificial watery cavern beneath the pavement. "You think her nose would let her survive with all those wonderful odors?"

At the same time that the streetlights flickered on, Daisy whipped around a corner and immediately froze. It was the first time she had stopped running through the labyrinth of streets and alleys since dashing away from Willie. There, just a few feet away, was the animal control van parked along the curb. Daisy knew she couldn't go back the same way she came—the dog gang was certainly on her trail. If she went past the van, Willie might see her since he could be sitting in the cab.

Daisy twirled her head around to find a place to hide. Then she saw an opening in the side and under the wooden steps of a three-family apartment house. She loped over and crawled inside. The stale air smelled of old, rotting wood. Several beams of light sneaked between the boards above her head and revealed a hard-packed dirt floor with a scattering of rusted soda cans. Daisy peered through a slit between the boards and noticed that the van's cab was empty. She took a deep sigh of relief. But before she could exhale, a door creaked. She glanced up through another crack.

To Daisy's horror, Willie came out of the apartment. He sat down on the steps, reached into his coat pocket and pulled out a package of cookies. Shock burst from Daisy's eyes when she saw up close that little beard glistening in the burnt, orange glow of the streetlight.

Willie bit into a cookie and a few crumbs trickled through the crack between the wooden boards and onto Daisy's nose. She held her breath and tried not to sneeze. Willie took another cookie and shoved it into his mouth. More crumbs fell onto the step near his feet and into Daisy's nostrils. She wriggled her nose—a sneeze was coming. Then she pushed her muzzle into the dirt to smother the sneeze. That worked—but not for long.

From the darkness, Daisy gazed up at Willie, who appeared to be staring right at her. The urge for Daisy to sneeze was stronger than ever. Willie craned his neck and looked closer at the step. Then he lifted a boot. The sneeze was wiggling its way up Daisy's nose.

She closed her eyes and tried to hold the sneeze one last time. She couldn't.

At the exact moment that Daisy's sneezed, a cricket jumped off the step and out of the way just as Willie slammed his boot onto the step. Her sneeze was drowned out.

Daisy held her breath again to listen. Willie dropped the rest of the cookie and squashed it with the other boot. Then he got up and walked down to the sidewalk. The van door opened and then slammed shut. The engine started and the van sped up the street. Daisy could breathe again. Willie was gone.

Later that same evening, Samson and the rest of the gang sat in a circle in the courtyard. They all looked downcast—and hungry.

"She's disappeared," Domino said in a slow, agonizing tone.

"We'll resume searching in the morning, the same way we did tonight," Samson said with a calmness that betrayed his seething anger.

But Georgie wasn't so calm. "And if we ever find her. Oh, beware! I'll...I'll..."

"Yeah, yeah, we know," Trapper said, unimpressed with Georgie's bogus angry rant. "You'll rip her legs off."

"You got it!" Georgie replied. "Those *real* long legs."

On the other side of the city, Daisy's faint outline was seen under a streetlight as she trotted down the street. Moments later she disappeared into the darkness.

Chapter Fourteen

Later that night, after journeying several miles from Cedartown, Daisy found herself in the midst of a cornfield. She knew she'd be safe for the time being, surrounded by countless rows of dried stalks that sheltered her from the cold wind that had whipped up across the countryside. She also reasoned that Willie would never think to search for her in such a remote place in the dark. Besides, she was too exhausted to go much farther. Now she could collect her thoughts and think about where she should go next.

Before she fell asleep on the soft ground, Daisy thought of Irving. She missed him even more. The effort that he had made to ensure her survival, especially since he never made it over the fence, seemed like a fading dream.

But what wouldn't go away was the nagging suspicion that somehow the kennel fire started because of the chaos caused by her escape. No matter how many times she had tried to justify herself, she always came back to the same conclusion: as soon as she escaped, the kennel burned down.

Daisy rolled up in a ball and made herself as small as possible to conserve body heat. Then her stomach rumbled. The steak that she ate had digested hours before. She knew she wouldn't have a meal like that for a long time.

The next morning, Daisy scampered from the cornfield and scaled a nearby hill to get her bearings. At the top, she gazed down into a broad valley rimmed with low hills while a hawk glided lazily overhead. The town that she had fled from the night before spread out in the distance. Just as Daisy was about to go back down the way she came, the beautiful sight of a white farmhouse with a wraparound porch in the foreground caught her attention.

As her eyes zeroed in on the farmhouse, the image of her ideal home soared back into her mind. What Irving had told her about Everett's home had created a picture of what she expected for herself. She had recited in her mind countless times that she wanted to find a house that had a huge yard with big trees around it. It would have nice people living there who would love and protect her and there would be toys to play with and a big, soft bed—and lots of dog treats, of course.

Daisy crouched in the tall grass and studied the farmhouse. A lush carpet of grass surrounded the house. Gigantic sycamores and red maples grew on both sides of a nearby gurgling stream that looped around the property. At the stream's high bank, Daisy noticed a five-year old girl with a pink ribbon in her hair, who was playing with her dolls. She sat at a miniature picnic table in the shade.

Then Daisy watched a woman carrying a basket come out of the house.

"Emily, do you want an apple?"

The little girl ran up to her mother and grabbed one of the fruit. A minute later, a red pick-up truck came into view from around a bend in the dirt road and pulled in front of the farmhouse. A man opened the door and stepped onto the gravel driveway.

"Mommy! Daddy's back."

Emily ran up to her father and hugged him. Together, they walked over to Emily's mother and the man kissed her. Then they all went inside the house. Daisy smiled and sprang to her feet.

"Wow! I sure hope they'll like me," she said out loud as she trotted down the hill toward the house. On her way down the slope, Daisy further imagined how she would soon be playing with Emily on a plush living room carpet—just like Everett had. Then Daisy thought how the father would come into the room and pour a bag of dog treats onto the floor and how she would dig her snout into the pile and gorge herself. After that, she would roll up into a ball on a huge cushion and close her eyes as Emily kissed her goodnight.

When Daisy came to the stream at the bottom of the hill, a short distance from the farmhouse, her ears shot up. A faint, distant whine—the whine of a dog that only another dog could hear—floated on the wind. Daisy bent down to drink but immediately raised her head when she heard the whine again. She cocked her head to one side and angled her ears. A breeze whistled through the tree limbs above and rustled the yellowing \leaves. Daisy lowered her mouth to the water again and lapped the clearest water she had ever seen.

Then she heard the whine a third time. It was louder and sounded agonizing. Gazing over wide-open pastureland, Daisy realized that there was a dog somewhere across it—a dog in extreme pain. Daisy turned and stared at the farmhouse and all the promise for a better life within its walls. Meanwhile, the faint whines continued. Emily would have to wait.

Daisy turned and bounded across the fields toward where she thought the whining might be coming from. At the end of the pasture, she passed through a strip of trees and leaped over a stonewall. As she emerged from the trees and landed on a dirt road, the dog whines became clearer.

Across the road stood an old barn, slightly tilted on its foundation. Many gray, wooden planks had been stripped off while several others dangled from the outside walls. Nearby, vines of poison ivy strangled a rusted tractor.

Daisy stuck her nose into the air and tried to pick up a scent. She smelled nothing and the whining had not resumed. Just as she was about to turn around and return to the farmhouse, a much louder yelp ripped through her ears. It came from inside the barn.

Daisy crept up to the barn doors, which seemed like they could drop off their rusted hinges at any moment. A steel pad lock glistened in the morning sun. It secured a thick chain that connected handles on both doors. Daisy poked the lock with her nose and sniffed all around it. It smelled of men—men who worked around dogs. As the handle rattled, another faint whine came from inside. Then she heard voices.

"Hey, Caesar, they're here. They shouldn't be this early."

"Maybe they're taking us out again," Caesar said. "But why this time of the day? Don't you find it strange, Brutus?"

Daisy squinted her right eye, closed the left eye and thrust her face forward until it pressed against a crack between the door and the frame. The barn was dimly lit inside but as her eyes adjusted to the dark, she could see several large dog crates scattered across a straw-covered floor. A couple fifty-five-gallon drums stood near the far wall. Above them was a narrow window, covered in cobwebs, from where blades of sunlight intruded into the barn.

There are dogs in those crates. Daisy thought. *What are they doing way out here?* She squinted again and made out the shape of a medium-sized dog. It had a wide face and an enormous black muzzle. The dog's cropped ears were folded back on its head.

"They're going to make us battle those thugs again," Caesar said. "Next time we should all attack those men. What do you say, Hannibal?"

"If we did that," Hannibal replied, "then what do you think they would do to all of us?"

Daisy steered her eyes to the other corner of the barn to see Hannibal. But she couldn't see him because of the angle.

"They would shoot us all, just like they probably did to Clipper."

Then Daisy heard a fourth dog.

"I wish they'd shoot me," he groaned. "I'm in so much pain."

"Attila, you'll probably heal," Caesar said. "But then you'll have to fight again."

"Why aren't they coming in?" Brutus asked. "I thought we heard the handle rattle."

Daisy stepped away from the door.

"Maybe it was the wind," Hannibal said. "Keep listening."

"No, someone had definitely tried to open that door."

They all became silent and waited. Daisy looked through the crack again.

"I see someone out there," Brutus said. "I can see a shadow blocking the light by the door."

"That's not a person." Attila pulled his head up from the wire mesh crate bottom. "It's another dog. I can smell it."

"Who's out there?" Caesar yelled.

They all waited for a reply. Daisy didn't answer back.

"Maybe it left," Hannibal said.

"No, it's still there," Caesar said, "because now I can smell it too."

Daisy continued to peer through the crack. She knew she wasn't in any immediate danger since the dogs were all shut up in crates.

"I see it," Brutus said.

"Me too." Caesar squinted his eyes. "Maybe he can help get us out of here."

"How's he gonna do that?" Hannibal asked. "He's locked out there and we can't open that door for him."

"Unless he can get in another way," Attila suggested.

Daisy wanted to run from there. Seeing dogs trapped in crates made her tremble. But one of them seemed like he was in severe pain and she didn't want to leave without trying to help him.

"Are you all right in there?" Daisy finally found the courage to speak up.

"It's not a he, it's a she," Hannibal said.

"Whoever you are," Caesar yelled out with a playful tone in his voice, "if you can break down that door and open up these cages, I think that would be enough."

"Why are you in there?" Daisy asked. "How many of you are there?"

"Four of us," Brutus said. "There were some others over the past few weeks, but they did away with them."

"Who did away with them?" Daisy tried to spot the speaker.

"The people who make us fight the Pit Bull Terriers—dogs just like us," Caesar said, now standing in his crate. "When the others got too badly beaten up, they took them out in the woods and who knows what happened to them."

Daisy was speechless. Her stomach began to hurt like it did when she found out that Greyhounds might be killed after leaving the track. She wheeled her body around and trotted away. There was no more room in her mind for terrible stories. She felt that these dogs would have to fend for themselves—she would have no part in risking her own safety for dogs she didn't even know. But she didn't get more than a few feet before she halted.

Chapter Fifteen

Daisy's heart felt like it had slumped into her stomach. *Why does it have to be this way?* she screamed inwardly. *Why are so many dogs kept in cages with no chance to live? I want to get out of here. I want to go back to that house.*

Daisy looked back at the barn door. She stared at the lock that kept those dogs from even smelling the crisp October breezes.

Daisy's head sagged as her thoughts went back to her racetrack days. She remembered Irving. His kindness to help her escape before they came to get her plowed away every selfish feeling she had. She imagined how Irving would react if he could see her walking away from a chance to save the lives of other dogs—dogs with no chance to escape on their own.

Seconds later, Daisy was back at the barn door. She again squinted her eye and looked through the narrow slit between the doors.

"Is one of you hurt?" Daisy asked as her eyes once more became used to the dark interior.

"Attila is," Caesar said. "He got torn up pretty bad last night. So did the other dog he fought. But they brought Attila back here and didn't even fix him up. We're afraid they're gonna come back and get him too."

"I don't know how I would ever get in there." Daisy looked up at the lock. "It's closed pretty tight."

"Go around the barn," Caesar said. "Look for some other door or opening. This place is real old. It must be falling apart somewhere."

Daisy backed away from the crack. She left the door and scampered around to the side of the barn. There were several broken windows but they were much too high to consider getting through.

When Daisy came to the rear of the barn, she noticed a crawlspace that led underneath. She stuck her head through the hole but hesitated to go farther. She could see her breath but the sunlight would only go a few feet into the damp, musty cavern.

Daisy took a deep breath, dropped onto her belly, and crawled into the space below the thick, rotting planks of the barn floor. After several feet of wading through dried mud and straw, she stood. Now her ears touched the beams above.

As Daisy was getting uneasy about being in such blackness, and was about to turn around and go back outside, she noticed a faint streak of light just beyond her. She shuffled toward it but her head slammed into a loose plank that hung lower than the others. Her forehead stung but she ignored it and pulled on the wood with her teeth. It broke off like wet cardboard. She grabbed another moldering plank next to it and yanked it off, leaving the rusted nails in the frame. Some of the boards had decayed so much that she was able to push her head up through the opening and into the room above.

"Now get the rest of you up here," a nearby voice said.

Daisy glanced around. Caesar's crate was just ten feet away. The fifty-five gallon drums stood next to the opening she had just created. She lifted her front paws onto the floor and hoisted her body up through the opening.

"Whew!" Caesar waved a paw in front of his nose. "It smells even worse down there than it does here. Now unlock these cages."

"C'mon," Hannibal said. "Let us out before they come back. They usually return sometime in the afternoon."

Daisy looked over at the injured dog.

"You really need to get help," she said. "You're bleeding from those scratches and bites."

"Who's gonna help me?" Attila asked. "I don't know why they didn't do away with me last night."

"You mean those men won't even try to help you?" Daisy examined one of Attila's front legs. The bite had gone all the way to the bone.

"Why would they?" Attila tilted his head as it rested on the wire floor. He looked into Daisy's eyes. "I'm surprised you would even come in here."

"We'll help Attila." Caesar winked at Hannibal and Brutus. "Just open all our crates."

"I guess you'll have to drop into that hole I made and crawl under the floor," Daisy said.

"Any way necessary," Caesar said. "Just hurry up."

"What are you waiting for? Are you scared of us?" Hannibal asked.

"I've seen some pretty mean dogs before."

"Were they fighting dogs?" Caesar asked.

"Well, yeah. They fought to survive on the streets."

"I guess you don't understand what we mean by us being fighting dogs," he said.

"Fighting is fighting," Daisy said. "Someone always gets hurt."

"What we mean," Brutus said, "is that we are set up to fight other dogs like us. People stand around and yell. The places we have to fight in are all smoky and kind of dark. Then, when a fight is over, they give each other money."

"So, they keep you here until you go somewhere else and fight again?" Daisy asked. "That's a horrible life."

"That's about it," Hannibal said. "They come here once a day to feed us and let us walk around the room. But they always close and lock the door before they do so."

"Can you open these cages now?" Caesar asked. "We promise we won't hurt you."

"Just pull out these bars on the doors," Brutus said. "That's how they open them. We just can't reach them."

As Daisy was about to unlatch Caesar's crate, all the dogs heard a vehicle humming in the distance. Daisy went to the door and peeked out. A jeep carrying two men quickly approached the barn.

"Aw, it's too late," Brutus moaned. "They're back."

"Maybe we can do it after they leave," Caesar said.

"You, whatever your name is," Attila said, not having the neck strength to follow Daisy as she moved about the room. "You better hide. You don't want them getting you too."

"Yeah, you better hide," Caesar said. "You're our ticket out of here."

"At least you'll get out of here," Attila said. "I know why they came here earlier." But no one heard him. The jeep's engine had drowned out his voice.

Daisy looked around the barn for somewhere to get out of sight. There was no place to crawl under. The barn was almost empty except for those drums, but they would not conceal her completely.

The jeep pulled up to the barn door and stopped. The engine shut off. Inside the barn, Daisy hopped up and down as she darted her eyes in every direction.

The jeep's doors opened and slammed shut. All the dogs lay in their crates and watched to see what Daisy would do.

A key was inserted into the lock. Daisy glanced back at the door. The lock opened and one of the men slipped the chain off the handle. The latch rotated. Daisy turned around and ran toward the hole in the floor. She was about to dive in, but then noticed that the drums that stood next to the opening had some space behind them. As soon as she squeezed in back of the drums, the door opened and brilliant sunlight filled the barn.

A man wearing a baseball hat entered the barn. Another man in a leather jacket followed, carrying a large bag of dried dog food and a gallon jug of water.

The men closed the barn door and then opened the crates. The three healthy dogs ran out and plowed their muzzles into the bowls of food that the men had placed on the floor. Attila tried to get to his feet. He dragged himself out of the crate but let out a yelp when he took his first step.

"Hey, Frankie, don't waste food on him?" the first man said. "We're not going to keep him around."

"I don't know, Butch," Frankie said. "I guess it was just out of habit."

Daisy noticed the distinct aroma of chicken as the dogs munched on the nuggets. Her stomach rumbled.

After the three healthy dogs had eaten their fill, they ran throughout the barn as usual to stretch their legs and get their blood moving. Attila finally made it to his bowl and began to eat. A bite mark on the side of his lip made it nearly impossible to take in more than one piece at a time.

After a few minutes, the other three dogs came together.

"You guys thinking what I'm thinking?" Caesar asked.

"You mean that hole in the floor?" Brutus glanced behind him at the opening less than ten feet away.

"It's staring at me and inviting me to come down," Caesar said.

"Can we all get through it before they try and catch us?" Hannibal asked.

"Maybe they got those guns." Brutus motioned with his head at the men near the far corner of the room.

"We have to take that chance."

"Let's do it," Brutus said. "They're looking the other way."

The three crept over to the opening that Daisy had made through the floor. The men remained with their backs to the dogs. One of them held a pencil and was writing something in a black pocket calendar.

Daisy peered from around the drum. Caesar noticed her and shot her an angry look.

"Couldn't you have just opened the cages when I told you?" he said. "Now we'll need all the luck we can get."

"Better join us," Brutus added. "Wanna have what's coming to Attila happen to you?"

Daisy glanced back at Attila. She looked at the hole in the floor and then at Caesar. She drew her body back behind the drum.

Hannibal shook his head. "You had your chance."

Caesar glanced at the men one last time and then dropped into the dark abyss, knocking two more boards down in the process. Hannibal quickly followed. The men turned around to see what the dogs were doing, suddenly aware that they hadn't been running around. They caught a glimpse of Brutus, just as the hole swallowed him up.

"Where'd they go?" Frankie asked as they ran over and peered into the blackness of the crawlspace.

"It goes to the cellar. Better get outside, 'cause they'll escape."

"What about him?"

"Attila?" Butch didn't even bother to look at the dog. "You know what to do to him."

Meanwhile, the men still hadn't noticed Daisy because she had squeezed her body behind the drum until she could barely breathe.

Butch leaped over a crate and hustled to the barn door. He threw up the latch and kicked the door open. Frankie reached into his leather jacket and withdrew a gun. Attila stopped chewing. He raised his eyes. Daisy saw the terror in his face. There was nothing she could do. She realized Attila knew what was coming.

Chapter Sixteen

"What's taking so long?" Butch asked, leaning his head back inside the barn. "Do it and let's go get the others."

"I can't. I just can't. Not when he's looking at me like that."

"I can tell you've never done this before. Forget it for now. I'll do it when we come back. Let's get those three before they get out of the cellar."

Frankie put the gun back into his jacket and rushed outside. The two ran around the barn to find the opening to the cellar. Too late. The three Pit Bulls had scampered out a few seconds before and were already racing down the road. The men sprinted back to the jeep and hopped in. The tires spun in the dirt as the vehicle peeled out and tore up the road after the escapees.

Inside the barn, Daisy dashed over to Attila.

"We gotta get out of here. Look, they left the door open."

"I can't walk much. It took everything I had just to get to the bowl."

"They may come back." Daisy's eyes switched between the wide-open door and the nuggets that remained in Attila's bowl. "Just try to stand."

"Ouch!" Attila cried out as he put weight on the injured leg. "It's so painful."

Daisy placed her head under Attila's chest and lifted him up. "Now take a couple steps. It'll get easier."

"Go...go get some of my food...if you're hungry. There's some left."

The Pit Bull favored his front paw and ambled toward the door. It started to bleed again. He stopped to lick it several times. Meanwhile, Daisy chomped down the nuggets—the most satisfying fifteen seconds she had experienced in a long time. A moment later, she rejoined her injured friend.

Attila hesitated. He glanced back at his crate. A look of deep sadness washed over his face. "Now I can go outside in the fields to die instead of in here."

"No. Just keep going. There's a stream near here. If you can get there, you'll feel much better. The water will clean your wounds too."

"I'll never make it."

"You will. I'll stay with you until you do."

"Why would you do this for me?" Attila asked. "Even my friends left me to die."

"I asked that question to myself once. Someone helped me to live, even when I didn't know I was in danger. He didn't have to do it, but he did."

The Pit Bull and the Greyhound left the barn. Attila hobbled onto the dirt road as Daisy steadied him with her body. Then Attila collapsed, raising a cloud of dust.

"Can't do it. I can't do it," he moaned. "Go on without me. Go back to your home or wherever you came from."

Daisy perked up her ears and made out a distant hum.

"Get up! Hurry! I think I hear them coming back."

Attila lay in the middle of the road. Blood oozed from his mangled leg. Daisy helplessly stared at it. The sound of the jeep was getting closer. Then she glanced into the barn. Without telling Attila where she was going, Daisy charged back through the door and ran to one of the open crates. She grabbed Attila's blanket and pulled it out. Then she dragged it out of the barn and placed it beside the fallen dog.

"Roll over. Get on this." Daisy nudged Attila with her forehead. "They're getting closer—just beyond that curve—I can see the dirt in the air."

"What good is this going to do?" Attila rolled onto the blanket.

"You'll see, now lie still." Daisy grabbed one side of the blanket and gave it a tug.

At first she could hardly budge it. But as she leveraged herself by keeping her body as low to the ground as possible, she managed to haul her companion to the side of the road. Just then, the jeep came into view about three hundred yards down the road.

Daisy let go of the blanket and took several deep breaths. Then she grabbed it again so her teeth could get a better hold. With all her strength, she pulled Attila farther away.

The jeep sped up the road and quickly pulled next to the barn. Both men climbed out.

"Three got away but this one won't," Butch said. "I won't have the cops wondering where he got all beaten up."

"But if they find those others, won't they start looking around for where they came from?"

"They can't prove they were used in betting. But this one is all chewed up. They'd know there was fighting going on."

Butch marched to the back of the jeep and grabbed a hunting rifle.

"Anyone hears a shot," he said with a wink, "they'll think we're just hunting for quail or something."

The two entered the barn. Their eyes searched for the injured canine. Then they looked at each other.

"He's run off too." Frankie looked back through the open door.

"He won't be too far," Butch said as he left the barn. "Probably hiding in the fields."

Frankie stepped onto the dirt road. "Hey, I found something. Paw prints lead into the brush."

"Let's follow it," Butch said, pointing. "He must be somewhere over there."

Meanwhile, Daisy had dragged Attila behind one end of the old stonewall. But the location wasn't far enough. There was still plenty of distance to the stream and the men had already started to comb the area. They searched under every bush and behind any clump of grass. Daisy guessed that they would find them in a short time.

"They're looking everywhere," Daisy said. "I'm going to distract them."

"Just save yourself," Attila said. "No use having both of us shot. At least it'll put me out of my misery."

"You can't give up this easily. These people use you just like others used me."

"But what else is there?" Attila writhed in agony as he tried to get in a more comfortable position. "This is all I've known since a puppy."

"There's a lot more." Daisy peered over the ivy-covered stones and saw the men wade through the bushes. "I'm going to find a good home over across this field. There's a house there with people that seem real nice. I'm sure they'll take me. Perhaps you'll find a home somewhere too."

"I hope they take you. You deserve it."

"Back where I came from, it wasn't a real home. The people there used to make me race against other dogs to get richer. Life was miserable most of the time."

"I had to fight other dogs I wasn't even mad at," Attila said as he bunched up a corner of the blanket with his paw to make a pillow. "There was this one time when I had to fight this other Pit Bull and we just stood there and stared at each other. Neither of us wanted to fight, but they forced us to. We had to fight and win or we wouldn't be fed. If we lost, it was usually because we were too hurt. Some healed right up, but others weren't so lucky."

Daisy never heard his last words. She had leaped from behind the stonewall. The men had come too close.

Chapter Seventeen

Daisy ran through the tangled maze of saplings and wild berry bushes. She crossed the road and dove into the tall grass behind the barn. When she got far enough away, she let out a howl. She forced as much pain into her cry so as to trick her pursuers that she was the injured Attila. It worked.

"He's over there," Frankie yelled.

The men sprinted past the barn.

"That's him." Butch pointed toward the field.

The grass parted as Daisy, unseen, torpedoed though the field. The men noticed the movement through the field and gave chase.

Again, Daisy whined as she led the men away from her new friend. As soon as they would get closer, Daisy would howl. Then she would sprint far enough away to give herself time to rest and allow the men to catch up. She did this several more times until she was clear across the pasture.

"Where'd he go?" Frankie asked when they came to the edge of the woods.

"Must've gone into the trees over there. Follow me."

Daisy veered off the road and cut across another part of the field. Five minutes later, she emerged on the front lawn of the farmhouse. She was proud of herself. Not only had she helped another dog escape and led his owners on a wild-goose chase, but she also had returned to her dream home. All she had to do was to let the people inside know that she was there and that she wanted to be part of their family.

Then a strange feeling came over her. The joy Daisy had expected as she was about to embark on her final steps to a life of love and acceptance had not come. And she knew why.

Daisy continued to stare at the house. She lurched forward but stopped after only two steps. There was nothing in her way that prevented her from exploding into a sprint and landing on the front steps.

Why shouldn't I make this my home? Daisy thought. *I deserve it. I spent a long time looking for a place like this.* As Daisy finished her thought, she discovered that she was gazing back over the pasture. Attila was still out there. Daisy had briefly forgotten about him. She recalled that he was far from the stream that she had told him about—and he would never get there on his own.

Daisy turned back to the farmhouse and stepped forward. Emily stood behind the screen door and stared at her. Daisy froze. Emily smiled.

No, I must take this chance, Daisy reasoned. *I'll never get another one. Attila will be fine once he gets some rest. His friends should be returning to look for him. They'll take care of him.*

But Daisy knew the truth.

Emily opened the screen door and walked to the edge of the steps.

"Mommy, there's a doggie watching me."

Her mother and father quickly joined her.

"I wonder where its home is?" the mother asked. "I don't think any farms around here have one of these."

"It's either a Whippet or a Greyhound," the father added. "I forget which one's which."

Together, the three crept up to Daisy, being careful not to startle her. Daisy desperately wanted to leap into their arms and forget about the past few weeks. She wanted to forget about all the mean dogs and people that had been in her life. She wanted to leave the hunger-filled days and bone-chilling nights. She would forget it all and begin a new life in the best home in the world.

The father bent over and rubbed Daisy's ears. Then he scratched her back from her head to her tail. Daisy couldn't recall so much pleasure.

"She's so friendly," Emily said. "I think she likes us."

"Could be a stray though." Her father took off his baseball cap and scratched his head. "Must've run off from somewhere."

"Can we keep her if we can't find where she lives?" Emily asked.

"Well, I don't know," her mother said, looking at her husband. "We don't know much about this type of dog."

"But we could learn—"

"Hold on, now," the father interrupted his daughter as he put his cap back on. "It came from somewhere so I wouldn't get your hopes up just yet."

Daisy glanced up at each person. They were all smiling as they looked down into her brown eyes.

She then turned her head and stared across the land toward the distant spot where Attila lay. She walked a few steps away and looked back at the family, then took a few more steps. Again, she looked back.

"You think she's going back home?" the mother asked.

"She's awfully dirty and scrawny to be owned by someone around here," the father said. "Maybe she's living in some hole out there."

Daisy turned and trotted toward the fields.

"Can we follow her to see where she lives?" Emily asked.

"Not if it's going to be too far." The father glanced down at his watch.

Daisy loped into the fields. The three jogged behind. Every minute or so, Daisy would pause to see where the family was and to allow them to catch up. A short while later, the old barn was in sight. Daisy cautiously approached it while keeping an eye out for the Pit Bull owners. She smelled the air. They hadn't returned yet, although the jeep was parked in front of the barn. The father shuffled around the jeep and peeked inside. Then they all looked through the barn's open door.

"Maybe she lives in here?" the mother asked, peeking inside.

"Could be." The father took a few more steps ahead of his wife and daughter. "But there are a lot of crates. Someone's been keeping dogs out here. I didn't think anyone had used this place in years. I'm going to call the police about this."

The father took out his cell phone and called the police as he looked at the jeep's license plate. Then he, his wife and their daughter investigated the inside of the barn.

Meanwhile, Daisy ran off into the fields to see how Attila was doing. She rushed behind the stonewall. Attila was still there, asleep. The blood on his leg had clotted but there were hundreds of flies swarming around his wound. Daisy bent down and licked Attila on the side of his face. He opened his eyes half way.

"Everything will be fine now, Attila."

The Pit Bull opened his eyes wide. They were filled with fear.

"You're not going to leave me out here to die, are you?" With little strength remaining, Attila lifted his head off the blanket. "I didn't mean it when I said I wanted to die. I want to live. Don't leave me. I still need your help."

"I won't leave," Daisy said. "You'll be all right soon. I have an idea. Maybe the people I told you about will take both of us."

A tiny smile poked out of Attila's face. He weakly wagged his tail as Daisy released a loud bark. The family heard the bark and ran from inside the barn. Daisy jumped on top of the stonewall so the family could see her. Emily saw Daisy first and pointed. Moments later they arrived to where Attila lay.

Daisy jumped back down, bent her neck and whispered into Attila's ear. "No more crates for either of us."

The mother and father gasped when they saw Attila. The father stepped over the wall and shook his head.

"Do they just let these dogs die out here?" He stooped and stroked Attila's back. Then he wrapped the dog in the blanket and picked him up. Daisy's tail rocketed back and forth as she followed the family back to the road.

Chapter Eighteen

When Emily and her parents stepped onto the road, they noticed the Cedartown animal control van parked in front of the barn.

"Wow, that was quick," the father said. "They even beat the sheriff out here."

"Daddy, what will they do with these doggies?" Emily looked at her father with a cheerless expression.

Emily's parents glanced at each other.

"Don't worry about this one, sweetheart." Emily's father gently placed Attila, still wrapped in his blanket, in the tall grass. "This one we're taking to the vet ourselves."

Meanwhile, Daisy had recognized the animal control van. She halted in her tracks just as Marty and Willie, who held the catchpole, emerged from the barn. Daisy's and Willie's eye's immediately met.

"Hey!" Willie lifted the catchpole like it was a battle flag. "Don't let that dog run off. She's a stray."

The father and mother glanced down at Daisy. She looked up at the father with sad eyes. The father appeared dumbfounded as Willie ran toward him. Daisy quickly slipped behind the father's legs.

"Grab her!" Willie shook his fist. "Do as I say and grab her."

Daisy darted away when Willie got within a few feet. Willie ran with all his might down the road after Daisy. But he tripped over the catchpole and fell. He got up and squeezed his fists just as a patrol car drove up.

"If you can run as fast as her," Marty said, chuckling, "then you're in the wrong profession."

Willie stomped over to Emily's father. "Why didn't you do as I said?"

"No wonder she ran off with you yelling like that. Now you'll never get her."

"Oh, don't you worry," Willie shot back as he turned to leave. "This is perfect. She's heading back to Cedartown."

Willie and Marty rushed back to the van and jumped inside. Marty started the engine even before the doors were closed. The vehicle's tires spit up clods of dirt as it peeled away from the barn.

Meanwhile, the sheriff and his deputy had parked their patrol car and had gone to investigate inside and behind the barn.

Frankie and Butch gave up chasing the dog they had thought was Attila and headed back to their jeep. On their way through the woods, Butch grabbed Frankie's arm. Frankie turned around to see Butch with his index finger over his lips and pointing toward a clearing in the trees. There, lying on a bed of moss, were the three other Pit Bulls.

So far, the dogs hadn't noticed the two men. Frankie and Butch crept closer, being careful not to make any noise. But Frankie stepped on a branch and the three Pit Bulls sprang to their feet.

"Get 'em!" Butch pushed Frankie ahead as they stormed into the clearing. "Grab 'em by the collars."

Caesar and Hannibal darted into the underbrush but Brutus had to avoid Frankie's reaching hand and ran in the opposite direction.

"Forget those two," Butch hollered, starting off after Brutus. "Get this one."

The men sprinted after Brutus through the woods and into the fields. Brutus saw the barn ahead and ran as fast as he could in that direction. But because Pit Bulls have short legs, Brutus was having a hard time maneuvering around the rocks, bushes, and saplings that dotted the old pastureland.

"I'll go around to the other side of the barn," Butch yelled out. "Just keep chasing him."

Although he was exhausted, Brutus managed to make it up to the crawlspace that went underneath the barn. He dove inside just as Frankie caught up to him.

But before Brutus could disappear into the darkness, Frankie grabbed his collar and yanked him back into the bright afternoon sunlight.

"Gotcha, big boy!" Frankie said playfully to the subdued Pit Bull. "We wouldn't want to be late for tonight's fight now, would we?"

Just as Frankie turned to head back toward the front of the barn, a burly hand grabbed his arm from behind. Frankie whirled his head and found himself face to face with the sheriff.

"No," the sheriff said in the same playful tone, "we sure wouldn't want him to be late."

Frankie automatically released the canine and threw his arms into the air. Brutus then ran into the crawlspace.

The sheriff shoved Frankie against the wall and clasped handcuffs onto his wrists. A moment later, a nose poked out from the crawlspace. The Sheriff looked down as Brutus ventured from the blackness. He lifted the dog to his chest. At the same time, the deputy came from the other side of the barn with Butch, who was also bound in handcuffs. The deputy smiled when he saw Brutus licking the sheriff's cheek.

"Weren't you telling me you wanted to get a Pit Bull some day?" the deputy said, as he thrust Butch against the barn next to Frankie.

Daisy skidded to a halt on the dirt road and looked behind. The animal control van was racing straight at her. But just before she took off again, Daisy peered far down the road, past the van, and saw the father carrying Attila. His wife gently stroked the dog's head as Emily skipped behind them. Daisy grinned— but just for a second. The van was getting too close. She dashed from the road, hurdled a clump of tall grass and disappeared into the brush.

Chapter Nineteen

By the next morning, a light frost had coated Daisy's fur. She had slept out in the woods and when she woke up, every muscle in her body screamed for warmth. Daisy quickly remembered Attila and thought how he must be sleeping under warm blankets in Emily's home at that very moment.

Daisy had come several miles since racing away from Willie at the barn, but now she was lost. She wondered if she should go back and find the farmhouse or, perhaps, start another search for a home.

Daisy got up from her bed of pine needles and ventured from the woods. A pasture opened up in front of her. She didn't have to go too far before she saw something that gave her a flicker of hope. To her amazement, the pastureland ended abruptly. Bulldozers had recently pushed up years of overgrown farmland. In front of her stood rows of houses that seemed to rise magically from the land. Several houses didn't even have grass planted yet. Everything smelled of new lumber. Daisy recalled the same scent back at the track when builders constructed a wooden shed near the kennel.

Before Daisy could leave the fields and cut through one of the back yards, movement from a nearby tangle of uprooted trees and bushes caught her attention.

Suddenly, Daisy heard muffled voices. The voices became louder and she realized that she had heard them before. Daisy's heart raced and she tried to hide. But it was too late.

"There you are!"

Daisy turned to her side. Caesar and Hannibal darted from behind a bush and jumped in front of her.

"Hey, you got away." Daisy backed up without taking her eyes off of the two Pit Bulls.

"After being hunted down like rabbits," Hannibal shot back.

"Those men probably caught Brutus." Rage discharged from Caesar's face. "Who knows what they'll do to him."

Caesar and Hannibal's eyes became slits as they slunk toward Daisy.

"If you had opened our cages in time, we all could've gotten away," Caesar added.

"But Attila, he—"

"Probably dead by now." Hannibal crouched low.

"And it's all your fault," Caesar said as he and Hannibal inched closer, forcing Daisy to back up even more.

Daisy retreated and collided with a tree stump entangled with wild blackberry branches. A thorn pricked her back leg, causing her to grimace.

The Pit Bulls stalked forward. They each opened their mouths, drool dripping, and showed their teeth and black gums. Daisy let out a whimper as her legs trembled.

"Why do you need to hurt me? I would've—"

"Let's just call it our duty." A sick-looking grin came over Caesar's face.

"You couldn't show us any mercy, so you get none now." Hannibal pretended to lurch forward, causing Daisy to spring backwards.

Daisy darted her eyes to find any possible way to avoid the attack she knew was coming. There wasn't enough room to slip to either the left or right of the two dogs. She was trapped. Then she had a last second idea. Daisy snarled and showed her teeth and pawed at the ground as if getting ready to charge.

"Hey, look who wants to fight back," Hannibal said with a crazy smirk.

"Then let's give her what she wants." Caesar also pawed the ground to mock Daisy's feeble effort to scare him.

"Let's get her!" Together, they lunged at Daisy. She waited until they were three feet from her. Then, with her powerful legs, she sprang high into the air. The Pit Bulls couldn't stop. They plowed into the tangle of thorn bushes.

"Ouch! It's ripping into my skin." Hannibal shook his leg to throw off the tiny barbs.

"Ignore it." Caesar grabbed a branch with his teeth that had whipped around his legs and cast if off. "She's getting away."

Daisy scrambled out of the thicket and tore through one of the yards until she came to a street. With many little daggers remaining in their flesh, the Pit Bulls charged after Daisy. She was more than a hundred feet ahead of them before she looked back. Her pursuers followed her with their noses to the asphalt.

As Daisy rushed up the road, she glanced into each yard for a place to hide. She quickened her pace and her eyes became wide with fear when she realized that many of the yards were fenced.

When Daisy came to the street entrance, she saw that there were no more houses beyond and that a busy street blocked her from going any farther. She looked down the street again. The two dogs fast approached.

With no time left to hide, Daisy bulleted up to the last house on the right. Her only choice was to leap over the fence and hope that there wouldn't be anything scarier on the other side. But just before she jumped, she noticed that the gate was already open a few inches. Daisy nudged the gate with her snout. It squeaked opened and she slipped through.

Daisy's eyes quickly spotted a place to hide. She burst across the lawn and scurried behind a juniper bush planted in a corner of the yard.

"She came in here," Caesar said as he and Hannibal skidded to a halt at the gate. "No doubt about it."

Hannibal stuck his nose in the air. "I smell her but I also smell some other kind of dog. Let's scram."

Caesar glared at his companion. "Remember who you are. We fear no other dog."

The two Pit Bulls marched across the yard. Hannibal then glanced to his side and noticed two enormous food bowls. He nervously prodded Caesar on the shoulder with his paw.

"Uh, Caesar, would that be dog or dogs?"

Caesar whipped his head around and stared at the bowls, at first appearing bewildered that a dog would need such a large bowl, let alone two.

"Forget it." Caesar turned back and pointed toward the bush. "She's got to be right over there. Oh, I can't wait."

"Maybe we should just leave." Hannibal tasted the air again.

"And you call yourself a fighter? Don't be such a coward."

Daisy shriveled in the corner against a stockade fence as she watched the Pit Bulls creep over to the bush. Just before Caesar and Hannibal came around to her side, Daisy dove under the bush.

"Get out of there," Caesar said through clenched teeth, "or I'll come in after you."

Caesar reached in with his mouth. Daisy pulled her foot back and let it snap. It belted Caesar on his jaw and he quickly pulled back out.

"Did you see what she just did? Now I'm really gonna give it to her."

"Just hurry," Hannibal said. "This yard smells creepy."

Caesar thrust his muzzle under the bush again. Daisy drew her feet in and tucked them under her hips.

Caesar grabbed her tail and clenched it between his teeth.

"All right!" Daisy squealed. "I'm coming out." Caesar let go and scooted out from under the bush. Daisy turned her body around and came out headfirst. Before she could get to her feet, both Pit Bulls pounced on her and forced her to the ground.

While Caesar pinned Daisy's neck onto the grass, Hannibal wrestled against her flailing legs. In a few seconds, Daisy's power was completely drained. She lay on her back and stared at Caesar. A smirk tore across his broad face.

"Now that we got your attention, I think there's this little matter about you not opening our cages."

"Get off of me," Daisy said, "or I'll really get mad."

"Ha!" Caesar laughed. "Now you're really scaring—"

Suddenly, Caesar took his paws off Daisy's neck and Hannibal hopped off her legs. They leaped over Daisy and huddled against the fence in the corner.

"Good thing you did," Daisy said as she raised her head and noticed the Pit Bulls shuddering, "because I wasn't—"

She was forced into silence when a huge shadow enveloped her. Then a deep growl, like the rumbling of a distant thunderstorm, sounded a few inches from her ear. She felt her heart melt inside her quaking chest. She slowly turned just as a deafening bark followed.

Chapter Twenty

Daisy looked up just as a Mastiff's enormous black figure lunged over her. The Pit Bulls bumped into each other to avoid a mountain of flesh about to crash on top of them. The two skirted out of the way and the Mastiff landed on empty ground.

Caesar and Hannibal tripped over roots and each other as they raced around the bush. The gigantic dog turned and leaped over Daisy again. Daisy twisted her head to follow the action. The Mastiff, with his jowls flapping, overtook Caesar and held his chest down with a monstrous paw. Meanwhile, Hannibal bolted back through the gate.

"Now, how do *you* like it?" The Mastiff clenched his teeth.

Caesar stared up at the two-hundred pound creature, whose snout was larger than the Pit Bull's head. Caesar could barely see the dog's eyes behind the thick folds of flesh.

"No!" Caesar wailed. "Please, don't hurt me."

Meanwhile, Daisy found the strength to stand up and watched from behind the bush.

The Mastiff barked again, which sounded more like a roar. "If I ever see you again in this neighborhood, maybe I'll do more than hurt you." The giant removed his paw. Caesar leaped to his feet and flew out of the yard.

The Mastiff watched until Caesar disappeared through the gate. Then he turned and looked at the bush. "It's okay," he said in a deep voice. "They're gone."

Daisy didn't respond.

"I'm not gonna hurt you. You can come out."

Daisy still didn't say anything as she peered through the leaves and branches. She had never seen a dog that large. He dwarfed even Samson.

The Mastiff thudded across the yard toward Daisy. The ground seemed to quake. By the time he came around the bush, Daisy had backed against the fence.

"Why'd you save me?" she asked.

The Mastiff's shadow quickly swallowed up Daisy's tiny frame. She almost forgot to breathe when she saw her rescuer up close. He had layers of flesh drooping from his jaws and an endless flow of glistening slobber oozing over them.

"They were in my yard," the Mastiff said. "Nobody like that ever comes in my yard."

"I—I had no—" Daisy choked on her words and let out a painful cough. Her neck still ached and her tail throbbed where Caesar had sunk his teeth.

"I didn't mean you. You don't have to be afraid."

Daisy struggled to get her breath back. "They would have killed me." She coughed again.

"It's okay, Buster won't hurt you. Buster doesn't hurt anyone."

Buster ambled to the middle of the yard. Daisy cautiously followed. Then she glanced at the gate.

"Good thing that gate was open."

"It's always open." Buster looked over at the gate and suddenly looked sad.

Daisy glanced back and forth between Buster and the gate.

"Don't your owners mind if you leave the yard?"

"I don't leave the yard unless I'm on a walk."

"If the gate is left open, other dogs might come in. Why do your owners keep it open?"

"They don't," Buster said. "I watched them open it one time and since then I just take my paw and do the same. It's easy."

Buster walked over to his water bowl. After taking three gulps he motioned with his head for Daisy to come and do the same. She ran to it and plunged her snout into the bowl.

With water dripping from the end of her nose, Daisy glanced back over to the open gate.

"I don't get it. Why do you want that gate open?"

Buster sat on the grass and rested his giant head on his forelimbs. "Have you ever been so lonely that you would do anything to get another dog's friendship?"

"I don't know what you mean." Daisy felt better as the cool water energized her. Then she plunked herself down on the warm grass.

"Would you believe that every dog in this neighborhood is petrified of me?"

"Look how big you are. Of course—"

"That isn't it. Look at my mouth. This white stuff just flows out constantly."

Daisy stared at Buster's face. "It's really not that bad."

"You don't think so? Watch." Buster stood up and shook his head. Drool splattered in all directions, much of it landing on Daisy.

"I see what you mean." Daisy chuckled and wiped her face on the grass.

"I hate going places in the car and I especially hate going for walks. The sidewalk gets wet from this stuff and all the other dogs snicker behind my back."

"Dogs that laugh at you aren't worth your friendship. You should ignore them."

"How can I ignore them? Just a few days ago, there were these two Cocker Spaniels staring at me and jeering. I turned right around and pulled my owner back here. He tried to hold me back but I gave him no choice."

"But what does that have to do with keeping the gate open?" Daisy asked.

"Hope. I always hoped that another dog like me might wander through. Maybe they would pick up my scent out on the street and know that another of my kind lived here."

"It's possible, isn't it?"

"I doubt it. It's been three years already and not once has another dog come though that gate—until today."

"I've never seen or heard about your breed," Daisy said. "Then again, every dog I met lately was a new breed to me. They even smell differently from my breed."

"I haven't even seen another Mastiff since I was a puppy." Buster lowered his head. "My owners don't take me anywhere where I can meet one."

"I kind of know what you mean," Daisy said. "I've seen a lot of dogs lately, but none of them were Greyhounds. It's just not the same, especially when I've lived my whole life with other Greyhounds."

"There must not be too many dogs like you," Buster said. "You're only the second one I've seen."

Daisy's ears shot up. "Second? Where'd you see another Greyhound?"

"Not too far from here. I was coming home from the vet some time ago and had my head sticking out of the car window. I saw a dog just like you—except she had gold colored fur."

"Which way?" Daisy jumped to her feet.

"You're going so soon?" A sadder look came over Buster's face.

"I'm desperate!" Daisy hopped up and down. "I need to find out how that dog found her home. This is another chance—maybe my last."

"I know." Buster dropped head. His forehead crumpled as he let out a deep sigh.

"Buster, I'm sorry. You have a home. I need one too." Daisy turned and headed toward the gate but stopped after a few feet. She looked at the gate. The Pit

Bulls had pushed it open all the way. She glanced back at Buster. His enormous head rested on his paws. They were wet. She wasn't sure if it was from drool—or from tears. She wandered back to Buster.

"I thought you were leaving," Buster said.

Daisy knelt on the grass beside him. Beneath the huge folds of skin, she saw a smile. She smiled back.

Buster told Daisy about his lonely life and how shy he had become because of the out of control drool. Then Daisy told him about her escape from the track and how hard it was to find a real home but also that she wouldn't give up looking. A short while later, Buster insisted that Daisy go on with her search.

"After you go out to the street, go right and keep going. But be careful, the streets get even busier." Then Buster gave Daisy a detailed description of the place where he saw the Greyhound.

When Daisy came to the gate, she paused. She turned back to Buster.

"What if your hopes and dreams are not inside here? Maybe they're on the other side of this gate. You'll never find out unless you go back out there and look."

Then Daisy bolted through the gate and disappeared from Buster's sight.

Chapter Twenty-One

In a few minutes, Daisy was far down the street and heading to where Buster had seen the Greyhound. Her body still ached from the tussle against Caesar and Hannibal, but she wouldn't let that slow her down. She soon came to a yellow fire hydrant in front of a small bakery.

Daisy recalled that Buster had told her that the Greyhound he saw was on the brick walkway that led away from the street—right where there was a yellow fire hydrant.

Daisy crept along the brick path to the rear of the bakery. The space between the buildings widened and she came to a large grassy area where the path split. She whirled her head around, unable to make up her mind which way to take. There were many staircases on either side and they each led to an identical brick townhouse.

"Do you know Milady? You kinda look like her."

Daisy almost jumped out of her skin. She turned and saw a Dalmatian lying at the top of the nearest set of steps.

"Milady?" Daisy asked. "Did I hear that right? There's more than one dog with that name?"

"She lives a few doors down. Moved in a couple weeks ago."

"Then she's gotta tell me how she found her home. Which house?"

The Dalmatian pointed with a paw. "That door with the flower boxes on the steps. She comes down this way every day."

"All by herself?" Daisy cocked her head. "Won't the dog pound people get her?"

"Oh, no, no, no. She's got an owner who takes her out for walks."

Daisy and the Dalmatian heard a door creak. They looked several townhouses away where a young woman leaned her head outside and reached into a mailbox fastened to the wall. Then the black nostrils and gold muzzle of a Greyhound stuck out from the doorway.

"That's a Greyhound! I'd recognize a Greyhound nose anywhere." Daisy thrust her snout into the air. "She also smells like a Greyhound."

Before the Dalmatian could respond, Daisy was already sprinting up the walkway. The woman's hand retreated from the mailbox with a bunch of letters. As the woman shut the door, she never noticed Daisy running in her direction. Daisy slammed her feet to a stop at the bottom of the steps and, to her surprise, she could see into the home through the screen.

Finally! Daisy said to herself. She clambered up the steps but knocked over a flower box. Dirt cascaded down to the sidewalk. Several rootless red petunias ended up draped over the top step.

The noise alerted the Greyhound inside the apartment. She came up to the screen and stared out at Daisy.

"It *is* you!" Daisy gasped.

"Well, well, well, Princess." Daisy's old rival stared out from the apartment.

"Milady? But how?" What are you doing here? Why aren't you at the track?"

"Look," Milady said. "You better not be seen around here. They capture strays right away."

Milady swiveled her head as footsteps thumped from inside the house.

"Get out of here," Milady demanded. "My owner's coming."

"No, I need to talk to you. Only you can tell me how I—"

"She's right in this room. Scram!"

"Wait!" Daisy pawed at the door handle. "When will you come out again? I can't wait much longer...it's cold...I'm hungry...I'm..."

A hand grabbed Milady's collar and pulled her away. The inner door slammed, the lock clicked and Daisy stood on the steps staring at the handle. She turned and hobbled down to the sidewalk. The Dalmatian joined her.

"She doesn't want to help me," Daisy said, looking downcast.

"Why not?"

"It's a long story. But I was so close just now. She said they'd get stray dogs. I'm so tired..."

"But she'll be out tomorrow if you don't see her today."

"I'm sick of tomorrows. I'll make sure I see her today. No matter what. Even it she still hates me."

The Dalmatian watched Daisy mutter to herself as she ambled across the street and into a small park. She slid underneath a bench that was surrounded by rhododendron bushes on three sides. From there she would wait until Milady's owner took her for a walk.

Then she would get her answer as to how to find a real home.

About an hour later, Daisy's head perked up. The sound of rustling—and sniffing—came from the other side of the bushes. She angled her head. The sniffing became more intense and followed the base of the bushes from one end to the other. Then, whoever was doing the sniffing, circled back.

Daisy squinted to try and see through the tangle of branches. She could barely make out a four-legged creature. Its feet were black—and huge. Her heart fluttered.

"Buster?" Daisy whispered. "Is that you?"

The sniffing stopped. She had been heard.

Daisy heart pounded harder as she watched the creature's paws. At first, the creature didn't move. Then, in a slow but determined manner, it circled toward the sidewalk. Then it came into full view. Daisy's eyes almost popped out of her head.

Samson!

"Aha! There you are. I thought I heard your little heart beating."

Samson then let out three earsplitting barks.

Chapter Twenty-Two

Many blocks away, Georgie was scrounging through a dumpster. He had momentarily became separated from Trapper, as each was hungry and wanted to search for a meal on his own terms. He lifted his head when he heard Samson bark. He tunneled back through the litter, jumped from the dumpster and scrambled off.

Domino and Harley were searching in an alley when they heard the bark.

"That's Samson." Domino's face shone with elation.

"Finally." Harley was already running down the alley and into the street.

In the back lot of a supermarket, Trapper was gobbling down pieces of thrown-out stale bread. He lifted his head when he heard Samson. He swallowed the food and rushed away.

Across from the park, an old woman sat by a window in her apartment. When she heard Samson barking, she craned her neck and pulled the curtains apart to see what was making all the racket. She saw Daisy and Samson.

"So many dirty, homeless dogs around here lately," she muttered to herself as she reached for a phone. "Can't those dogcatchers do their job right?"

Samson stood above Daisy, who remained trapped under the bench. He seemed much larger than before—and she felt much smaller.

"Finally, gotcha," Samson said with snarl. "When the others get here, we'll all deal with you together."

"Why, why, why!" Daisy moaned as a couple tears slid down her cheek.

"Crying's not gonna help. Criminals like us forgot what pity is." Samson tightened his jaw and pushed out his chest.

But to Samson's amazement, Daisy stopped weeping. And, to add to his surprise, a furious look swept across Daisy's face.

"You're criminals because you're cowards," Daisy bellowed.

"Cowards?" Samson roared back. "You're the one hiding."

"You're all cowards because *you've* given up. "

"Wha—"

"You're scared to find a good place to live." Daisy's furious tone momentarily made Samson speechless. "You steal and fight instead of finding a home where someone will love you. In a town like this there are hundreds of chances. I just lost my dream home but I still won't give up."

"What if I don't want a home?" Samson shot back with even more intensity in his voice. "My home is all around me. After we punish you, we're going to force you to join us, then you'll have the same thing."

Samson twisted his head and looked over at the townhouses. He and Daisy saw a car pull up to the curb. A young man stepped out. He climbed the stairs and entered the apartment where Milady lived. Daisy's eyes widen. She guessed that in a short time, Milady would be going for a walk since over the past few weeks she had watched how dogs would be taken outside soon after their owners came home.

Samson turned back to Daisy and gritted his teeth. "I told you that I had a home in this city once."

"Why would you give that up? What could be worse than barely surviving in those stinking alleys?"

Samson was forced into silence. He lowered his head and, for what seemed like an eternity, he didn't move. Then, to Daisy's astonishment, a tear escaped and ran down his cheek. Another quickly followed. Daisy had to shake her head to make sure she wasn't imaging what she was seeing. This was the powerful, terrifying Samson?

Daisy stared at the spot where the tears had dripped onto the sidewalk. For several moments, neither dog said anything. Finally, Samson found his voice.

"You want to know what's worse than living in these filthy alleys?"

"There's nothing." Daisy shook her head. "A home has warm beds, it has people who will love—"

"Wrong!" Samson got down on his haunches and stared into Daisy's eyes. "It's living in a house where you're kicked and yelled at all the time. Oh, I know *all* about what you're looking for. I had a home like that for three years until…"

Again, a tear slipped from Samson's eye and trickled to the end of his nose.

"…until the boy who I was given to as a puppy had gone off with his mother. They never came back."

"Where'd they go?" Daisy asked, softening her voice.

"I don't know. But as soon as they left, the father would yell at me for anything I did. He would sometimes even throw shoes at me."

"That's horrible."

"Uh-huh. But you know what was the worst thing he did to me?"

Daisy shook her head.

"He ignored me." Samson let out a deep sigh. "Yeah, I was fed once a day, but no one ever gave me love and attention like that boy did. When he left, a part of me died."

"How'd you know he wasn't coming back?"

"Every once in a while, when the father came home, I smelled that boy on his clothes. For some reason the boy wasn't coming back. He didn't want to see me and I never knew why. I guess he just didn't love me anymore."

Daisy gazed at Samson with a tinge of sympathy as she soaked in his painful history.

"But I know he did love me once," Samson continued. "When I was a puppy, he would hold me in his arms and show me to all his buddies..."

Daisy watched a sparkle of happiness twinkle in his eyes as Samson went on with his story.

"...but the best thing was when he would take me to this pond and he would try and catch frogs but I would scare them into the water. Then he would point at me real seriously and pretend he was mad at me. But then he would burst out laughing, so I knew he... Hey, why am I telling you all this?"

Daisy shook her head. "Then how'd you end up on the streets?"

"C'mon, what's with all the questions?" Samson gave Daisy an irritated look. "If you really have to know—one evening, my owner took me for a ride. Then he stopped at the end of some dark street. He took off my collar and opened the car door. He let me out and then...he...he drove off. He just drove away. I waited all night there, just in case he..."

Samson's forehead crumpled. He turned his face away, too embarrassed at having Daisy see him so upset. All Daisy could do was to stare back in disbelief.

"No one ever came looking for me," Samson continued, as he fought to hold back more tears. "And I never found the boy, even though I used my nose to try and pick up a scent, but I couldn't—"

Suddenly, the townhouse door opened. Daisy and Samson again turned their heads. The young man stepped out leading Milady on a leash. Daisy's mouth opened as she watched. Then she and Samson lifted their ears. From a distance, they heard Domino and Harley calling for Samson.

"They'll be here in a minute," Samson said so quietly that Daisy barely heard him.

"I feel sorry for you. I'm the one trapped here, but I feel sorry for you, and for your buddies."

Samson stood. He paced back and forth as he looked at Daisy. She stared back, confused.

"Get up! Go!" Samson gazed up the street. "They'll be here any second. Get outta here and find your home."

Daisy squeezed from under the bench. She saw Domino and Harley trotting up the road in the distance. Trapper joined them from a side street.

"Run as fast as you can." Samson gestured with his paw in the opposite direction from where the other gang dogs were running. "You're too good to stay in a place like this."

"But—"

"Run!"

Daisy spotted Milady and her owner turning a corner. She was about to dart after them, but paused. She turned back to Samson.

"Don't give up. Go back to your old home. See if that boy came back. You never know."

Daisy sprinted off after Milady and was quickly out of sight.

Moments later, Domino, Harley, and Trapper skidded to a halt at Samson's feet.

"You got her?" Domino asked, out of breath.

"Nah, false alarm." Samson still stared to where Daisy had vanished around a corner. "I found a dog I never knew before."

"Then where'd it go?" Harley darted his eyes around the bush.

"I hope she finds what she's looking for." Samson released a smile.

"Samson," Trapper said, giving him a funny look, "you're talking crazy."

"Yeah...hey, where's Georgie?"

All four dogs exchanged worrying looks.

At the same time, the animal control van rolled to a quiet stop on the other side of the park. Inside the van, Marty ran his finger down a sheet of paper.

"Brown and white female Greyhound," he said, as he hung up the two-way radio.

"That's the one!" Willie rubbed his hands together. "That's definitely her."

"Great. Let's bring her in. Then I don't have to listen you gripe about your lost hound anymore." Marty tossed the paper to Willie. "Gotta look for a Rottweiler too."

"I'm taking the pole this time," Willie said as they exited the cab. "You take the harness."

"Wait a second." Marty scowled. "You're telling me what to do—again? You almost strangled that poor Husky the other day."

"I need that pole, Uncle Marty. Aren't you concerned about my career development?"

"Here's your career development." Marty thrust the harness into Willie's chest. "You can go search around Main Street. I'll look around the park."

Meanwhile, on a nearby street, Georgie anxiously glanced around as he pitter-pattered along the sidewalk.

"Samson?" he cried. "Hey, Samson, where are you?"

Chapter Twenty-Three

On Main Street, Daisy saw Milady and the young man stroll up the sidewalk about a block away. Daisy quickened her pace as she called out.

"Milady, wait, wait!"

Milady apparently didn't hear. But someone else had heard Daisy barking. She whipped her head around as footsteps got louder and louder behind her. Willie had spotted Daisy and was now in a full sprint. Daisy stared back, stunned. But only for a second. She broke into a run and scooted away toward Milady, who had disappeared among the throngs of people.

Back at the park, Marty had seen Samson and was now running after him. His hands squeezed the catchpole as his rotund body undulated over the grass. Samson then stopped. Marty extended the pole toward Samson's head. The dog jumped aside and the pole smacked the ground.

"Here I am," Samson barked, sticking his tongue out. "Here I am."

Marty turned around. He took another swipe at Samson but missed again. Then Harley sneaked up behind Marty.

"And I'm over here."

Marty heard Harley barking and rotated his torso. He swung the pole but Harley easily escaped the noose.

All four dogs played with Marty like moths around a light bulb. Marty's pole became heavier and heavier. Then the pole dropped out of his hands while chasing Trapper. Marty tripped over the pole and crashed to the ground. He was panting like he had just climbed Mount Everest. He sat up in the grass and watched the dogs race off in the same direction that Daisy went.

Over on Main Street, Daisy zigzagged through a swarm of pedestrians. Her eyes darted back and forth as cars whizzed by. She looked behind. Willie struggled to get through the crowd. With Willie distracted, Daisy decided to cross the street to shake him off her trail. She took a step into the road. A car honked and she pulled her foot back onto the sidewalk. She spun around and sprinted farther down the sidewalk. Then she spotted Milady while her owner chatted with another man in front of a store. Daisy rushed up to Milady.

"Finally!" Daisy glanced in back of her one more time. "I've been searching for a home and haven't spoken to another Greyhound since the track. You have to help me."

"Why should I help you?" Milady said with a huff. "You tricked me. You played a joke on me. You—"

"It's so cold at night and there's nothing to eat."

"Maybe you deserve it."

"C'mon, Milady. I need help. Please."

"All right, just to get you off my back. You gotta find the Greyhound place."

"The bad place where the racetrack dogs go? Or the dog pound?"

"No, the place where the dogs find new homes. If you can get there, you'll be sure to get a new home."

"How do I get there?" A smile streaked across Daisy's face."

Then Milady eyes bugged out as she looked over Daisy's shoulder. "There's that awful man from the track. Is he after you?"

Daisy whirled her head around. Willie was jogging toward her. "Oh, no! Help me. Where's that

Greyhound place? He's gonna take me to the dog pound."

"Straight down this road." Milady pointed with her nose. "Maybe you'll smell other Greyhounds."

Daisy darted away just as Willie rushed up. But a bicyclist rode into Daisy's path. She skirted to the side to get around. Too late.

To Daisy, it seemed like a bad dream as the harness flew over her head and neck. Her heart froze as she gazed up into Willie's face. Willie clasped the harness under her chest and fastened the leash.

"None of my dogs *ever* get away from me." Willie did a little dance while winding the leash around his wrist a couple of times. "Never, ever."

He took out the piece of paper from his pocket. His hands trembled like a man who had just found a gold nugget. He struggled to hold Daisy and the paper as he folded back Daisy's ear. Inside her ear were several tattooed numbers—just like all racetrack dogs have for identification.

"Just making sure," Willie said. "We wouldn't want to disappoint Mr. McKenzie now, would we?"

A happy smile appeared on his reddened face.

"Can't believe I got her!" Willie said over and over as he led Daisy back to the animal control van.

A few minutes later, he opened the back doors and Daisy jumped in without hesitation. Willie unhooked the harness and then slammed the doors shut.

He was about to get into the cab when he heard a rustling noise coming from behind a newspaper box. He tiptoed away from the van.

As Daisy lay on a black wool blanket in the rear of the van, the reality of her capture began to sink in. Just as the first teardrops cascaded down her long nose, she was startled by a scratching noise coming from under another blanket near the front of the cargo area. A small white face emerged.

"It's scary, isn't?"

Daisy didn't respond as a dirty mutt with tangled fur came out and sat a few feet from her.

"I mean, not knowing where they're gonna take us."

"I know where I'm going," Daisy said. "To the dog pound. They finally got me."

"How'd you end up out here?"

Daisy lowered her head. "Didn't I deserve a nice home like other dogs? I was so close. So close... I raced to find happiness but lost."

"Yeah," the mutt said. "I've had a hard life too."

"I've never had a life. Those people always banging on the crates, yelling at us to go out, or come in, day after day. Then, when we raced, we were all petrified that we wouldn't do well enough. We never knew what day would be our last."

"Just horrible."

"And the worst thing was knowing that we had to leave our friends. I left someone who cared about me deeply. I'll never see him again."

"Who was that?"

Daisy closed her eyes and rested her chin on the blanket. "Ever since I escaped, I've thought of Irving constantly. He loved me."

The mutt sighed. "At least you had someone who cared about you. The only attention I got was rocks thrown at me or kids kicking and chasing me."

"I saw so many dogs living in homes, playing out in their yards or going for walks. I always wished it could be me."

Daisy burrowed her nose and head between her outstretched forelimbs. The mutt went back to his blanket. A couple of tears flowed down his face.

Several yards from the van, Willie crept up to the newspaper box. He stooped and reached behind a pile of crumpled newspapers. Out came Georgie.

"Would you be so kind to join us?" Willie asked the trembling Chihuahua.

He stuck the dog under his upper arm and returned to the van. He opened the back doors and tossed Georgie into the cargo area.

From a short distance away, Samson and his gang had watched Willie catch Georgie. Samson narrowed his eyes and released a low, ominous growl.

Inside the van, Daisy lifted her head. "They got you too?"

"Oh, help me! Help me!" Georgie pleaded. "I need Samson. Help me!"

Before Willie could close the doors, Daisy stood up and stepped to the doorway to have one last look at her freedom.

"Where do you think you're going?" Willie pointed his bony finger at Daisy's face. "Go lie down. Now!"

The mutt came next to Daisy and peeked out.

"Stay, you mangy hairball. You'll have lots of company soon."

Daisy glanced down at the mutt. He gave her a weak smile and went back to lie on his blanket.

Meanwhile, Samson and his gang slunk low and quietly as they crept closer to the van.

Willie was about to slam the van doors, but Daisy's nose stuck too far out the back. Then she stared into Willie's eyes.

"What," Willie said with a snarl. "You need some persuading?"

Daisy suddenly recalled when she struggled to get over the fence back at the track. She thought about how Willie had held her hind legs and how much that hurt. Then she remembered how Willie had kicked Irving—that angered her the most.

Daisy furled her brow. In a flash, she leaped onto Willie. They both tumbled to the pavement. Georgie and the mutt rushed to the edge of the cargo area and watched Daisy claw at Willie's head. He let out a scream and shielded his face. Then Daisy nipped at Willie's flailing arms. He squealed and flipped over onto his stomach.

Then, as quickly as she had attacked, Daisy pounced off Willie's back and raced off. But she didn't get far. Samson and the gang blocked her way.

"Wow!" Trapper's eyes seemed to explode off his face. "What a gift."

"Let's get her before that guy gets up." Harley had already moved toward Daisy.

Samson immediately thrust his paw against Harley's chest and showed his teeth. "She's not the one we want."

Chapter Twenty-Four

Willie sprang to his feet and rushed back to the van. Georgie and the mutt retreated farther into the cargo area. Willie slammed one of the doors. Then he grabbed the other door handle. Just as he was about to shut the second door, he heard a chorus of snarls. Willie slowly turned around. Samson and his buddies methodically closed in on him.

"Uh, good doggies." Terror filled Willie's eyes. "Oh, are you looking for your friends?"

The dog gang wasted no time. They all pounced on Willie and knocked him down. Then they went to work on him, tearing at his clothes as he tried to fend them off.

"Uncle Marty!" Willie flopped on the pavement like a seal. "Help me!

Samson then dug his teeth into Willie backside. Willie let out a scream.

"That one's for Georgie."

Georgie and the mutt stuck their heads out from the van. They both grinned at each other and then jumped onto the pavement just as several people rushed over to watch the action. Milady and her owner also saw the commotion and ran over.

One woman, apparently distressed over how the dogs were shredding Willie's clothes, yelled out, "Maybe someone should call animal control."

"That *is* animal control," Milady's owner replied.

At that moment, Marty staggered back to the van with one hand grasping his heaving chest. The other hand dragged the catchpole. Samson and the dogs noticed Marty and halted their attack. Willie saw his chance to escape the battering he was receiving. He sprang to his feet and dashed for the safety of the van, leaving strips of clothing peppering the pavement. He got into the cargo area and slammed the doors shut.

Meanwhile, Daisy had watched the action for several seconds and then realized it was time to get away. She glanced around, trying to get her bearings. Just as she turned to bolt up the street, she saw Milady pointing with her paw.

"Not that way, Daisy! It's the other way to the Greyhound place. Down this road."

Daisy nodded and raced off.

Back inside the van, Willie grabbed the mutt's blanket to cover his head. But just before he did, something got his attention. He opened a small wire mesh door and crawled into the cab. Through the windshield, Willie saw Daisy running off.

Outside the van, Marty realized the dog gang was closing in on him. He backed up to the van and reached for the door handle. But just before he opened the door, the van roared away from the curb.

Marty cupped his palms over his mouth. "From now on, you're going to clean the dog crates back at the pound! You hear me? I'll take someone else with me on these patrols."

Marty suddenly found himself surrounded by six dogs. Each one showed his teeth as they stalked the unlucky man. One by one, each dog faked an attack. Marty whimpered with each pretended assault. It was all a game to the dogs.

"This is great!" The mutt hopped up and down in pure bliss. "Mind if I join your gang?"

"What do you say, Samson?" Domino asked. "Can he come?"

"Maybe he can join you, guys," Samson replied while gently petting Georgie's tiny head. "I've got a boy to find. Georgie, you coming?"

Willie steered the van around cars and rifled through an intersection along Main Street. Daisy looked over her shoulder. Her eyes widened when she realized Willie was gaining on her. She sped up. Willie then released a sinister-sounding laugh as he got closer to Daisy. He was a man possessed.

Then Daisy remembered what Milady had told her about smelling other Greyhounds. She halted, shot her muzzle high in the air and took a big whiff. A gentle breeze floated across an open field along the road. And then she smelled it—the faint, yet distinctive scent of Greyhounds. *Where's it coming from?* Daisy thought. *Which direction should I run?*

Daisy looked farther down the street. The congestion lessened as the road left the city. There would be no way she could outrun the van heading in that direction. Then she turned to the left to where an abandoned factory stood. *Would Greyhounds be kept in there?* Daisy whipped her head to the right and gazed across the field to where a green building stood surrounded by a seven-foot brick wall. Then she looked behind. The van was almost at her. No more time to think.

Daisy wheeled her tired body around and tore across the field.

Willie jumped the curb and drove the van into the field. As the van got closer to Daisy, clouds of dirt trailed both dog and vehicle.

Daisy kept her eye on the brick wall. It drew nearer. Willie accelerated and brought the van alongside her. Then he slammed on the brakes and the van skidded to a stop. He flung the door open and bolted after Daisy. His fingers became white as he squeezed a leash.

Daisy glanced behind and gasped.

With the brick wall almost upon her, Daisy felt as if her legs were hauling rocks. She knew she couldn't keep the pace up for much longer—this was worse than any race at the track. Willie was just a few feet behind with his arm already extended to grab Daisy's harness. The Greyhound pushed off the ground with each stride. But it wouldn't be enough—or would it?

Just as Willie was about to seize the harness and to finally subdue the weary dog, Daisy leaped. The brick wall loomed above her. She extended her legs and stretched her body. Willie reached up, his fingers ready to clasp. Daisy's forelimbs hooked the top of the wall while her hind feet pushed off the bricks. For a split second, Willie's face shone with delight as his hands closed in on Daisy's back legs.

Too late. Willie grabbed air instead as Daisy scaled the rest of the wall and disappeared onto the other side. Willie couldn't stop and smacked into the wall. He bounced off and slumped to the ground. He briefly raised himself up and then fell back down while rubbing his forehead and sobbing like a child who had just dropped his ice cream cone.

On the other side of the wall, Daisy plunged onto the grass and rolled twice. She stood up, stumbled a few feet and then collapsed—too exhausted to move. She realized she was trapped in an unknown place and it could only be a matter of time before Willie found her again.

"I'm sorry, Irving." Daisy's mouth barely moved as she spoke softly through the blades of grass. "I didn't make it." Then she closed her eyes.

Chapter Twenty-Five

Suddenly, a shadow fell over Daisy's face. Her nostrils twitched as she picked up a familiar scent.

At first, he didn't recognize her. Her eyelids were crusted up with dried tears, and mud was caked between her toes. Several ribs could be seen protruding under her flaky skin. Daisy lifted her head slightly and squinted. The sun hurt her eyes.

"Daisy?" Now she heard a familiar voice. "Can it be...is that you?"

Daisy raised her head higher and rapidly blinked. Then she exploded to her feet as energy surged back into her body.

"Irving!"

Daisy's mouth hung wide open but no more words would come. She danced on her toes while Irving's tail rocketed back and forth.

"I never thought I'd see you again!" Irving said.

"But where am...how'd you..."

"Where are you? You just crash-landed into the best place in the world!"

Daisy sobbed and laughed while a wide grin streaked across Irving's face.

"You're...you're alive!" Daisy couldn't stop hopping up and down. "The fire...the fire that night... How'd you..."

"Calm down. Calm down." Irving caressed Daisy's cheek with his snout. "I'll tell you in a moment. I just can't believe it's you and—"

"I want this to be true. Oh, let this not be a dream." Daisy shut her eyes tightly for several seconds and then reopened them.

"It's a Greyhound rescue shelter," Irving said.

"Then I made it!" Daisy's tail wagged explosively. "I really made it! I had the most horrible time. I barely got away from that man from the track just now. But how'd you get here?"

"The dogs were brought here after that fire. I didn't think you knew about the fire. I thought you were far into the forest."

"It tore me apart not knowing what happened to everyone." Daisy reflected for a moment. "I watched it all burn and thought you may have all died."

"It seemed the track people thought we were too spooked from what happened that awful night. So they brought us here."

"But how'd everyone get out? There was all that smoke and—"

"We all worked together. But Tommy and Spencer were real heroes. They kept going back inside that burning place to bring every dog outside. After that, we were taken into those vans and brought here. For some reason, the woman at this shelter didn't let anyone adopt me."

"Adopt?" Daisy released a flabbergasted look. "What's that?"

Irving then told Daisy how the news somehow had quickly spread that a large group of Greyhounds needed homes. People and families would come and play with the dogs. After a while, they would choose a Greyhound and take it home. Tommy, Casey, Spencer, Max, Milady, Teddy—Irving went through the whole list—were all given homes in a matter of days.

"Then maybe Max was *wrong* about them killing all the dogs," Daisy said.

"Especially since I smelled Dalton here and I think I even got a whiff of Jasper and some of the other dogs—but not all of them. We may never know for sure, but hopefully they all were adopted. I wish we had known this would be the place they'd take us after the track. Then the future wouldn't look so scary. It's not knowing what's in store for us that's so terrifying."

Daisy nodded. Then a somber look came over her.

"Did you smell your sister in here? Please say you did."

"No..." Irving sighed and hung his head. "I never smelled Priscilla. I sniffed all around the yard...everywhere...not a trace."

"I want to stay with you." Daisy sat down on the grass next to him. "You cared about me and I didn't deserve it. I embarrassed myself over Tommy and now I realize I didn't really... Well, all I know is everyone could have died because of me."

"Don't think that way."

"Somehow that fire started because I—"

"You have to listen to me." Irving gently raised his voice.

Daisy got quiet and stared at him.

"Your willingness to escape," Irving continued, "and to try and find a better life helped the rest of us find happy homes—although in a very strange way."

"Who'd ever imagine?" Daisy smiled and slowly shook her head.

"From the day you arrived at the track, I knew you were special. I loved you but couldn't tell you until that very last day."

"But why?"

"I never thought you could love me in return. You were so beautiful and—"

"But I do love you, Irving. These past weeks made me think about how much you did for me. I still can't believe I fell for Tommy's games. I know he saved a lot of dogs, but why do some of the dogs act like him—or Milady?"

A sad look swept over Irving. "It's hard for any of us to really be ourselves when we're stuck in crates all day and kept only to race. I was at the track longer than most, so I could see the difference. When the dogs came to the track for the first time, they were more themselves. But many would eventually change and become either selfish or arrogant."

"But *you* were never selfish," Daisy said. "You were doing your best to save me from being taken away. I was the one that was selfish and didn't deserve having you risk your life for me."

Irving smiled and kissed Daisy with his wet nose and then they cuddled.

Suddenly, the back door of the green building opened. A woman appeared in the doorway. Daisy jumped to her feet.

"Relax," Irving said. "She's just the owner of this place. She's real nice."

Then the silhouette of another person appeared behind the shelter owner. Daisy got a worried look, which turned into panic.

"Oh, no! That must be the awful man from the track. What am I going to do now?"

Irving sprang to his feet and showed his teeth. "I won't let him do a thing to you."

Daisy quickly skirted behind him to hide as the shelter owner walked down the stone steps and into the yard. Then the other person came into full view.

"Oh, yes!" Mrs. Clark floated down the steps. "That's definitely her—the wonderful dog who found my handbag."

"Funny," the shelter owner said, giving Daisy a puzzled look. "I wonder how she got in here?"

Mrs. Clark skipped across the grass toward Daisy and Irving. Daisy ran over and met her half way. Irving quickly followed. Mrs. Clark knelt and stroked Daisy's ears.

"Wow!" she said. "I finally found you. Will you come home with me now?"

Daisy's face shone with joy as she savored the soft tone of Mrs. Clark's voice. But then she looked at Irving. A look of sorrow came over him. Daisy turned back to Mrs. Clark and gazed sadly into her eyes. Mrs. Clark reached over to Irving and stroked his chin. Then she drew both dogs closer to her and gave them a tight hug.

"But a home with one dog is just a house." Mrs. Clark glanced back at Daisy. "Will your friend also come with us? I have two wonderful children who would love a couple of companions. How would both of you like some playmates?"

Daisy and Irving locked stares and gave each other a wide grin, apparently understanding Mrs. Clark's intentions.

"I wanted to keep this gentle guy with me," the shelter owner said. "I now see that these two are definitely attached—it even seems like they know each other. I think they'll be happy together."

Daisy and Irving followed Mrs. Clark and the shelter owner into the building. The two Greyhounds kept looking at each other and shaking their heads as if what they were experiencing was almost too good to be true. The shelter owner took Mrs. Clark and the dogs down a hall and to the front of the building where the office was.

As Daisy and Irving continued to share smiles, the shelter owner abruptly stopped. Mrs. Clark bumped into her, while the two Greyhounds plowed into Mrs. Clark.

A man stood at the front desk.

"Can I help you, sir?" The shelter owner appeared stunned as she scanned the man from top to bottom.

The man whipped his head around.

This time it *was* Willie. His uniform was in tatters, the bruise on his forehead had become the size of a lemon, and he was covered with dirt.

Willie gritted his teeth and venom shot out from his eyes as he pointed at Daisy. "That dog will be coming with me now. "

The shelter owner and Mrs. Clark looked at Willie in shock, then at each other, and then back to Willie.

"Didn't you hear me? Hand her over!" Willie took a couple steps forward.

Mrs. Clark glanced down at Daisy and Irving, who both were looking up at her with fear in their eyes. The shelter owner, still stunned at Willie's appearance, struggled to respond.

Suddenly, Mrs. Clark brushed past the shelter owner and stood in front of her.

"You made me lose this precious dog once. I will not allow this to happen again."

"She's my dog. None of my dogs—"

Mrs. Clark marched up to Willie and thrust a finger against his chest. He stumbled backwards until he slammed into the shelter entrance door.

"If you think you're going to take her away from me—"

"Lady, you don't know what..." Willie felt for the door handle.

Mrs. Clark folded her arms and squinted. "Show me the proof of your ownership of this dog."

"The tattoo in her ear... umm... Mr. McKenzie will..."

The shelter owner regained her composure and came and stood next to Mrs. Clark. "I know Mr. McKenzie. He already signed all of those Greyhounds to us. You can't fool me with that."

Mrs. Clark's face became red as she came nose to nose with Willie. "Go back to the pound and never let me see you near this dog again."

Willie threw open the door and tumbled down the steps. He got right back to his feet, threw up his arms in defeat, and tramped back to the van, which was still parked in the field. He never looked back.

Daisy and Irving each released a huge sigh.

A half hour later, after all the paperwork was completed for the adoption of Daisy and Irving, both dogs sat on the back seat of Mrs. Clark's car. Suddenly, the windows rolled down as the car left the driveway and sped up. Daisy immediately recalled the Afghan Hound that had stuck his head out the car window back at the racetrack parking lot. She sprang to her feet, thrust her head through the window and allowed the wind to tease her ears while she let her tongue dangle. Her eyes shone with happiness as the car zoomed along the road. Irving noticed what Daisy was doing and then jumped up and did the same out the other window.

Both dogs' heads jutted out of the car on the way to Mrs. Clark's home. Then Daisy noticed Buster lounging in front of his house on the grass. Another large dog, a Great Dane, sat next to him. Daisy barked. Buster glanced over at the car. When he recognized Daisy he cheerfully barked back.

Chapter Twenty-Six

The next day, Mrs. Clark pushed open a screen door with her elbow as she carried a tray with a ceramic pitcher and four mugs onto the raised deck behind her gorgeous colonial-style house. A thick curl of steam rose from the pitcher as she set the tray onto a table next to where a forty-year-old man sat in a wicker chair. The man took off his reading glasses and set aside a newspaper while Mrs. Clark filled each mug.

"Matthew...Hannah!" Mrs. Clark called out. "Come get your apple cider while it's still hot."

A plush carpet of Kentucky blue grass spread a couple hundred yards from the house. A twelve-year-old boy and an eight-year-old girl took turns tossing a rubber chicken to Daisy and Irving. When the children heard their names, they ran across the lawn and up the stairs to the deck.

The two Greyhounds continued to play with the toy chicken. Each took turns flipping it in the air while the other caught it. When it was Irving's turn to catch it, he let it flop onto the grass next to his toes. Daisy noticed that Irving was gazing across the yard with a distant look in his eye.

"I wish I could find Priscilla," he said after a moment of reflection.

"Maybe we will one day." Daisy gave Irving a reassuring nod.

Irving nodded back. "Maybe... Hey! How 'bout we race? Down to that fence."

"I don't know," Daisy said. "After being forced to race all that time, I think it's killed any desire in me to—"

"C'mon, there's nothing more to be afraid of now. Nothing."

As Daisy looked over the yard, a smile scurried across her face. "Then, to the fence!"

The two dogs took off and barreled across the grass. Irving glanced over his left shoulder, expecting to see Daisy falling behind. But then a blur blew by him on his right side. Daisy sprinted ahead and reached the fence first. When Irving caught up, he kissed her on the nose.

"You're home, Daisy. You're finally home."